STRANGER IN TOWN

Cheryl Bradshaw

Copyright © 2012 by Cheryl Bradshaw
First edition November 2012

Cover Design Copyright 2012 © Reese Dante
Interior book design by Bob Houston eBook Formatting

ISBN: 148020725X
ISBN-13: 978-1480207257

For updates on Cheryl and her books:

Blog: cherylbradshawbooks.blogspot.com
Web: cherylbradshaw.com
Facebook: Cheryl Bradshaw Books
Twitter: @cherylbradshaw

Also by Cheryl Bradshaw

Black Diamond Death, (Sloane Monroe Series #1)
Murder in Mind (Sloane Monroe Series #2)
I Have a Secret (Sloane Monroe Series #3)
Sloane Monroe Series Boxed Set (Books 1-3)

Whispers of Murder (Novella)

Grayson Manor Haunting (Addison Lockhart Series #1)

*The first chapters of all Cheryl Bradshaw's books
can be read on her blog*

DEDICATION

This book is dedicated to anyone who has ever lost a child.
My heart goes out to you.

ACKNOWLEDGEMENTS

To my husband, Justin, for his unwavering support—and for helping me understand things like guns, wild animals, and fishing. You still owe me a pistol, by the way.

A big thanks to Dr. Brian Reedy at the School of Chemistry and Forensic Science in Australia for answering my forensics questions.

Many thanks to the best editor and gal around, Janet Green (thewordverve), my formatter, Bob Houston, and my superb cover artist, Reese Dante.

Thanks also to Becky Fagnant and Amy Jirsa-Smith, my proofers.

To my friends and family for your continued support.

And finally to Tracy Chapman. "The Promise" is the theme song for this novel.

"At what point shall we expect the approach of danger?
By what means shall we fortify against it?"

-Abraham Lincoln

CHAPTER ONE

Pinedale, Wyoming
October 17, 2010

Six-year-old Olivia Hathaway tiptoed down the center aisle of Maybelle's Market, stopping once to glance over her shoulder and make sure her mother wasn't watching. But Mrs. Hathaway was too engrossed in selecting the right card for her sister's birthday to notice her daughter had slipped away.

Olivia looked left and then right before scooting one aisle over. She peered at the products lining the shelves and then shook her head. "Nope, not this one."

She frowned and moved on.

The colors from the paint samples on the next aisle were like bright strips of candy, beckoning her to come closer. So she did. She loved plucking the cardstock strips from their slots and adding them to her collection at home. She'd gathered so many over the past few months, her mother had bought her a notebook to glue them all in.

The star-shaped colors were Olivia's favorite because they weren't plain and ordinary like the rectangle ones, and they had fun names like "Summer Sparkle" and "Twinkle, Twinkle." She tapped her pointer finger on the top of each card like she was playing a game of "eeny meeny miny moe" and then selected her favorite color: green. She'd always wanted a green room, but her mother said green was for boys and had painted Olivia's room pink instead.

Olivia held the green star out in front of her and twirled around and around, fascinated with the glitter that had been mixed in to the paint. If only her room could be as beautiful as this. Maybe if she wished hard enough, one day, it would be. She kept that thought in her mind as she spun around one last time before she collided with something hard.

"Hello, Olivia," a man's voice said.

A man in a black ball cap and mirrored sunglasses smiled and pointed at the ground. "You dropped something."

Olivia froze.

"Here, let me get it for you," he said.

The man scooped up the painted star and held it out in front of Olivia. "Go on, take it," he said. "Don't be afraid."

Olivia didn't know why her stomach felt like a bunch of ants were crawling around inside, but she did know the way it made her feel: scared. She wanted to shout for her mother, but when her mouth fell open, nothing came out. She looked down at the ground, hoping when she looked back up, the man would be gone. But he wasn't.

"Come here, sweet thing," the man said. "It's okay. I don't bite."

When Olivia didn't move, the man knelt down in front of her. He lifted up her stiff body and set her down on his knee. "Do you want me to take you back to your mommy?"

Olivia squeezed her eyes shut, but when she opened them, the man's hands still wound around her tiny arms like a boa constrictor. *If he wants to help me find my mommy, why is he holding me so tight?*

"How far away is your mommy?" the man said.

Olivia pointed.

"How about this—give me a hug, just a little one, and we'll look together." He held a finger out in front of her. "Pinky promise."

Olivia wanted nothing more than to be back with her mother again. The man's breath smelled like her mom's when she hadn't brushed her teeth in the morning. Olivia leaned in just enough for the man to hold her close, but jerked back when the mountain of stubble on the man's chin scratched her face. She knew her cheek wasn't on fire, but it burned like the metal from a seat belt on a hot day.

The man patted Olivia on the back and stood up. "There now, take my hand."

Olivia looked down. Her fingers were clenched in a tight ball, the edges of her untrimmed nails digging into the soft skin of the palm of her hands. She stuck out her tiny hand, and the man wrapped it in his. But when they got to the end of the aisle, he didn't turn toward where Olivia had pointed, he kept walking.

A faint whisper echoed in the distance. "Olivia, honey, where are you?"

She wanted to cry out, "Mother, I am here!" But the man clasped her hand so tight, she was too afraid to say anything.

Hand in hand, they walked through the front door. The sun had just started to go down when they stepped outside, but it was still light enough for Olivia to recognize the person walking toward them.

"Olivia, is that you?" the woman said.

It was her white-haired, wrinkly-faced neighbor, Mrs. Schroeder.

"Excuse me," Mrs. Schroeder said to the man, "I don't believe we've met. I'm Helen Schroeder. Are you a relative of the Hathaway family, in town for a visit perhaps?"

The man looked down and kept walking without responding to the old woman. He stopped next to a silver car and turned to Olivia. "Get in."

She did.

He shut her inside and turned around to find Mrs. Schroeder glaring up at him.

"I really must insist you answer my question," Mrs. Schroeder said. "Or I'll have no choice but to call Olivia's parents right now."

Mrs. Schroeder tapped her wooden cane on the back window of the car. "Olivia, dear, do you know this man?"

The man glanced around. Seeing no one, he pulled a knife from his front pocket, clicking a button on the top. The knife sprung to life. Before the old woman had the chance to scream, the man thrust the knife into her side. "I'm sorry, but I've had enough of your stupid questions," he said.

The woman tried to grab for the door handle, but

collapsed to the ground. The man stepped over her and got into the car.

Olivia shielded her eyes and thrashed her head from side to side. "It's okay, everything's okay. Mommy will find me," she whispered to herself. All she could think about was being at home in her pink room. If she could just go home, she'd never run away from her mommy again.

The man started the car and backed out. The car bounced up and down for a moment. It reminded Olivia of the time her dad ran over the neighbor's cat by accident. Olivia gathered up enough courage to move one of her fingers away from her eyes just enough to see Mrs. Schroeder through the car window. She was on the ground, motionless.

The man turned around, smiling. Olivia noticed a hole in his mouth where a tooth should have been.

"Mrs. Schroeder will be okay, Olivia," the man said. "She fell down, that's all. Lie down now, and try to get some sleep. When you wake up, you'll be home."

Olivia stared down at her star, wishing what he said was true.

Inside the store, a frantic Mrs. Hathaway ran up and down the aisles begging anyone she came in contact with to help find her missing daughter. A few minutes later the store was locked down. But it was too late. Olivia was gone.

CHAPTER TWO

I-80 Freeway, Eastbound
October 9, 2012

No matter how hard I tried, I couldn't peel my eyes away from the digital numbers on the dashboard clock in front of me. It was 12:45 p.m., and I had two options: break the law by speeding or accept the fact I was going to be late. I glanced around, taking in the reflection of the rear-view mirror, and slammed my foot down on the pedal.

Two hours earlier I'd been enjoying a cheese soufflé with my friend Maddie when my cell phone rang. I hadn't recognized the number and sent it to voicemail. But something about seeing the little white number "1" circled in red on my iPhone sent my OCD into overdrive. Turning the phone over and setting it down on the counter didn't help things either. I knew when I flipped it back around the number would still be there, taunting me like a baker dangling a fresh, glazed donut in front of my face. *Take it, you know you want to.*

So I did.

The message began, *Hi, umm, my name is Noah Tate. I got your card from someone I met. I'm looking for a private investigator, and he recommended I contact you. If you're not too busy, I'd like to meet later today. I realize it's short notice...*

There was a moment of silence, and then ...

Please. If you could just help me. I don't know what else to do.

It was Saturday. My day off. I had a policy about not taking new clients on the weekends. It was how I convinced myself I wasn't *really* a workaholic. But something about the way the man's voice cracked in between his words intrigued me. He was desperate, and I wanted to know why.

When I called back, the man wouldn't say why he wanted to hire me. He just said he'd rather not discuss it over the phone, and asked if we could meet in Evanston, Wyoming in two hours, a place just past the Utah border. Although it was less than two hours away, I'd never been to Wyoming in my life.

I exited the freeway in Evanston and searched for the restaurant that Mr. Tate had described as log-cabin style. In a sea of fast-food joints, it wasn't hard to find. An eight-foot tall carved moose kept watch out front. Only a few cars were parked on the lot, one of them being a vacated black Dodge Ram with an expensive, after-market grill on front. It was flashy, and polished to a buff shine. Content with my Audi, I'd never fully learned to appreciate trucks before, but this one demanded it.

Across the street at the McDonald's, a young mother and her two boys sat at a table beneath the golden arches. One of the boys shoved a fry in each one of his nostrils and made a face at his mother, who wasn't fazed in the least. Not to be outdone, the other boy sucked some soda through a straw and ejected it. The liquid landed on a pile of chicken nuggets she was eating. The boys giggled until their mother gave them a look all mothers give when they're about to go McCrazy.

I reclined my seat back and closed my eyes. Some time later, I woke up and looked around. There was no sign of Mr. Tate or his beige SUV anywhere. *How long had I been out? Fifteen minutes? Thirty?* It felt like an hour. I glanced down at my phone. Forty-five minutes had gone by.

I checked my text messages and had received one written in all caps: BE THERE SOON, NOAH TATE.

I never understood what compelled a person to show up late without any regard for the person they'd inconvenienced. I dialed Mr. Tate's number. It went to voicemail. "Wait fifteen more minutes," I said to myself, "then leave."

Fourteen minutes later, I turned the key in the ignition and put the car in reverse, almost backing into the beige SUV that whizzed across the intersection and into the parking lot at warp speed. The vehicle jerked to a stop, and a slender, red-faced man with no hair to speak of opened the door and scurried out. He smoothed some crumbs off of his expensive-looking, button-up shirt, glanced around, and advanced in my direction.

"Mr. Tate?"

The man nodded, sticking his hand through my open

window.

I didn't take it.

"Call me Noah, please."

"You're late," I said.

"I'm sorry. I sent you a text. Didn't you get it?"

"That's your excuse: 'you sent me a text?'"

He shrugged. "I tried to leave on—"

"Call next time," I said. "Or I might not be around when you get here." I got out of the car. "Should we go in?"

He nodded and followed me inside.

The waiter seated us at a wooden table with legs made of thick, knotty logs. Black and white photographs were haphazardly glued along the top and had been covered with some type of lacquered glaze, sealing them in place. The photographs looked like they'd been taken several decades earlier and showed what the town was like before it turned into what it was today.

Once we were seated, Mr. Tate looked both ways before sliding a bank envelope over to me. The look on his face made me feel like we were making a drug exchange. I took the money, setting it to the side. I hadn't agreed to anything—not yet.

"I'm not clear about why you wanted to hire me," I said. "I need to know before I accept the job."

"I didn't want to discuss it over the phone."

"Why not?"

He tapped his pointer finger on the table and whistled a few notes from an unfamiliar tune. "It's not an easy subject to discuss in front of my wife."

"Your wife isn't here now," I said.

I thought about all the reasons a man would need to discuss something away from the watchful eye of their suspicious spouse, the most prominent being cheating or something having to do with money. But Mr. Tate didn't appear to have money problems, and he didn't seem like the unfaithful type either. Then again, the best cheaters never did.

"It's not what you think," he said.

I shrugged.

"How do you know what I think?"

"You wrinkled your face just now like I've done something wrong," he said. "I haven't."

"I'd like to know why I'm here."

He leaned back in the chair, laced his fingers together, and rested them on the edge of the table. "A couple years ago a young girl named Olivia Hathaway was kidnapped a few hours from here."

The name seemed vaguely familiar. "Where was she taken?"

"From a grocery store in Pinedale."

"Is Pinedale in—"

He nodded. "Wyoming, yes."

"What happened?"

His shoulder bobbed up and down.

"No one knows for sure. They were shopping at the time, the girl and her mother. Her mother remembers telling Olivia to hold on to the side of the cart while she looked at something, but when she turned back around, Olivia was gone. She searched every aisle with the store employees, but found no sign of her anywhere."

"They never found her—dead or alive?"

He shook his head.

"Police combed the area, formed search parties, and put her picture up on every post, billboard, and store window. By the time they were through, they'd gone over every inch of Pinedale at least once. There wasn't a soul in the state of Wyoming that didn't know the girl was missing."

"And there were no witnesses?" I said.

"None that lived to talk about it."

I sipped my water.

"So there was someone who saw what happened?"

"A store employee discovered an elderly woman dead in the parking lot right after Olivia was taken. She'd been stabbed once, and then run over."

"By a vehicle?"

He nodded.

"A car."

"She must have seen something," I said.

His demeanor conveyed much more than a person who was sharing a story. He was connected somehow.

"Is Olivia your daughter?"

He swallowed hard and glanced out the window.

"I'm sorry," I said. "I can't imagine how hard it would be to lose a child."

A single tear formed in the corner of his eyelid. He quickly swept it away. "Olivia Hathaway is not my daughter."

I set my glass down and looked up. "If she's not your daughter, why are you here and why tell me this story?"

"My daughter's name is Savannah," he said. "Savannah Tate."

CHAPTER THREE

"Savannah Tate—of course," I said.

He perked up.

"You've heard the story then?"

"Everyone has," I said.

Savannah's abduction took place at a preschool in Jackson Hole, Wyoming, six months earlier. Once the media got a good whiff of what had happened, things spun out of control. Finger-pointing and blame spread in all directions, most of it resting on the shoulders of the daycare itself. No one working that day understood how they had managed to lose a child—from an enclosed play area, no less. Even more bizarre was the fact that Savannah hadn't been outside alone. She had been playing with another child who was the same age, leading to even more speculation. People wondered why they weren't both taken, why one had been chosen over the other.

The daycare employees were interviewed on WNN, Wyoming's nightly news, each one tearing up on camera, but an unsympathetic public didn't care. A toddler was missing because of the daycare's mistake. It might have been an honest one, but it didn't stop parents from pulling their children out of A Place to Grow Child Care Center until no children remained. Soon after, the child-care center was forced to close. A rumor circulated about a twenty percent decrease in daycare attendance across the nation. Mothers from every walk of life clutched their children a little closer that week, opting to find what they felt were more "suitable" arrangements. Many turned to in-home child care, thinking their children were much better off in the comfort of their own homes.

Two weeks after Savannah was kidnapped a new website sprung to life called All Kids Safe. It was a place where parents could hand-pick quality nannies in their area. All employees had to undergo a background check and adhere to a code of ethics. The idea of children getting personal care made parents feel safe, making All Kids Safe a huge hit.

"I hope you understand now why I wanted to wait until I could speak to you in person," Mr. Tate said. "My wife doesn't even get out of bed anymore. She's tired of...well—everything. The media coverage, the constant interviews by the police, the ladies on the street bringing casseroles over every night. She can't take it anymore, and neither can I."

"How's the investigation going?"

"Seems like they've done more harm than good. We've been given the same statistics so many times now, I can quote them for you."

When I failed to respond in a timely manner, he backed up his statement.

"Every forty seconds a child is reported missing or abducted," he said, "eighty-two percent by family members, many taken within a quarter mile of the child's home. Seventy-four percent of children who are murdered are dead within three hours of their abduction."

I stayed quiet. He kept going.

"Why do they tell us this stuff? Do they really think it makes us feel better to hear it? I'm aware of the statistics."

"I believe they're just trying to be realistic. The last thing they want is to give you some sort of false hope. It may seem harsh, but it isn't. They just want you to know the truth."

"I'm not some delusional parent asking you to look for his daughter when there's a good chance she's dead," he said. "She's still alive—I know it."

I thought about how many times I'd watched parents on TV say the same thing. Admitting a loved one was gone wasn't easy. But now wasn't the time to explain everything police officers and detectives went through as a team when something of this magnitude happened. He wasn't healthy enough to hear it yet, let alone understand.

I removed a pad of paper and did what I do best.

"Is there a specific person working with you—a detective maybe—someone who keeps in touch more than the others?"

He nodded.

"There's a detective. Name's Walter McCoy."

I jotted it down.

"McCoy makes a lot of promises, but there's no delivery," he said. "McCoy says he'll keep looking even if it takes the rest of his life, but if you ask me, he's headed toward retirement.

Why would he stay committed? It's not like his daughter was taken."

"I'm sure he doesn't see it the same way."

"What do you mean?" he said.

"You have no idea how many cops have 'the one.'"

"What one?"

"The one they never solve," I said. "It's something they carry with them their entire life. It's not some itch they can scratch to make them feel better. It's always there, in the back of their minds. Even when they sleep, they have nightmares. It doesn't ever go away."

"McCoy never tells me what he's been up to, how much time he's spending on my daughter's case, nothing. What am I supposed to think?"

"Maybe there are facts about the case that haven't been revealed to you yet," I said. "When the time is right, they'll fill you in. I know it's hard right now, but you have to be patient. I'm sure they're doing the best they can."

"I'm done being patient," he said. "I've been interviewed so many damn times, it seems like my wife and I are their only suspects. They waste time talking to us when they should be finding our daughter."

"Cases like this add a lot of pressure for everyone involved," I said. "The public often pushes police, demanding answers, and when they don't come—well—you can see how stressful it can be, right?"

He tilted his head slightly. "I don't know—I don't trust them. And now there's this new guy in town."

"A cop?" I said.

He shrugged. "Not sure. McCoy just said he brought him in to work on the case, so it didn't get 'cold.'"

"Do you have a name?"

He shook his head.

"Don't know, don't care."

"I'm surprised this new person hasn't met with you yet," I said.

"He tried."

"And you refused?"

"Why would I want to start working with someone else at this point?"

You'd think he'd be willing to work with anyone if it led to finding his daughter.

"You could at least give him a chance."

He swished his hands through the air like he thought I was crazy. "He's just another person working for *them*. I want someone working for me." He aimed a thumb at himself.

I felt like I was missing something important, something he hadn't said yet. It didn't sit well with me.

"Is there anything you haven't told the police?" I said. "Because if there is, I can't take your case unless I know about it."

Noah leaned back in his chair, placing one of his hands on his forehead like he'd just been stricken with a massive migraine. "Before I answer, I need to know one thing: Do you believe there's a chance my daughter is still alive?"

Statistics weren't in his daughter's favor, but numbers had never meant much to me. "I believe you think she is, and that's enough for me."

Noah closed his eyes and smiled. "Good. I want to show you something."

CHAPTER FOUR

Flattened on the table in front of me was a piece of paper. A princess resembling Sleeping Beauty frolicked in the middle of a field of flowers, all of them pink. In fact, the entire page was pink. I lifted the piece of paper up and examined it. There was no writing of any kind, just outside-of-the-line scribbling done with a waxy Crayola.

"What is this?" I said. "I mean, I can see it's a torn page from a child's coloring book, but where'd you get it?"

"In the mail."

His tone of voice had changed so much one would have thought I was holding a newly discovered artifact.

"When?" I said.

"Three days ago."

"If you're showing this to me, obviously it means something to you," I said.

"I believe it was colored by my daughter."

I stared at the picture, not knowing what to think. Could it be possible?

He grabbed the paper, waving it back and forth in front

of me. "Don't you see what this means? She's alive!"

Or someone had a twisted way of turning a wayward parent into a believer.

"Why haven't you shown this to the police?"

He leaned back in the chair and crossed his arms. He had a smug grin on his face like my astute observation had impressed him.

"What makes you think I haven't?"

"It's still in your possession," I said. "If you would have handed it over to Detective McCoy, it wouldn't be."

"You're right. He would have taken it from me and said something about how it needed to be 'entered into evidence.' I'd never get it back. You have no idea what this means to me—to my wife. It's—helping her cope."

I understood the attachment he'd formed and why, but he wasn't doing himself any favors by hanging onto it.

"You don't know what they'll do until you show it to them," I said.

"Olivia Hathaway's parents got one too. They handed it over, and once the investigators all looked at it, her mother asked if she could have it back. What do you think they said?"

Now I understood why he'd taken the time to mention the other kidnapping; if both parents received the same type of correspondence, the kidnappings could be connected.

"When did Olivia's parents receive their coloring page?"

He leaned in. "Last week. And do you want to know what the cops did with it? They published it in the local paper. Why the hell would they do that?"

"It's a new lead. Olivia has been missing for two years.

Maybe they're trying to generate some interest."

"I always thought the kidnappings were connected," he said. "McCoy looked into it, but he never found any evidence to support my theory, other than the fact both girls were taken from the same part of Wyoming. When I received the coloring page in the mail, I found out where Olivia's parents lived and paid them a visit. Imagine how good it felt to know they'd received one too. I've been right all along."

"I don't mean to sound callous Mr. Tate, but how do you know this isn't someone's idea of a sick joke?"

"Mrs. Hathaway said Olivia's favorite color was green. The page they received was full of stars, all of them colored green."

"What's the significance of the star?"

"Apparently Olivia had some kind of glow-in-the-dark solar system on the ceiling of her bedroom, and green was her favorite color."

"And I'm guessing Savannah's room is pink and princess-themed?"

He nodded.

"It must have been checked for fingerprints," I said.

"Olivia's parents said when the prints were processed the only ones they found besides theirs were Olivia's. They checked the envelope it was sent in too. There were no prints that couldn't be accounted for."

I held the page in front of me. "Mr. Tate, you have to turn this over to the investigators working on your case. You can't keep it."

He slapped his hand against the side of the table. "I will

not!"

"This coloring page is the one thing connecting both abductions to each other. Can't you understand why the police need to be informed? It will give them the first solid lead they've had in months."

He shook his head. "You don't get it. I don't care about Olivia's case. I mean, of course I feel sorry for what her parents are going through, but my only concern right now is finding my daughter."

I pressed my pointer fingernail into the pink wax on the page. "I'm sure you can't see it right now, but you're hurting your chances of finding Savannah by hanging on to this. I understand what it means to your wife, but you need to listen to me."

He threw both of his hands into the air. "I thought if I paid you to do a job, you'd have to do things my way. I'm the client. You work for me."

I pushed my chair back and stood up. "I work for myself. And I don't appreciate you treating me like I'm some factory worker you can order around just because you're waving a wad of cash in front of my face."

"Now, hold on a minute. Listen—"

Breathe, Sloane, breathe.

"No, you listen. If I agree to take your case, and by 'agree,' I mean, I make the decision—not you—I'll stick with it until it's solved or I'm certain there's nothing else I can do. You can take it or leave it, but I'll tell you one thing—you'll never find another PI with the same kind of devotion that I have."

The way his face twisted up while I talked told me he hadn't been spoken to that way by a woman very often, if ever.

"Wow, you sure think a lot of yourself, don't you?"

"Here's how it works with me," I said. "If I decide to take your case, you'll comply by doing exactly what I want you to do when I want you to do it. You have the right to refuse, giving me the right to walk away. I will never ask you to do anything that isn't in your best interest. And if you want my help finding out what happened to your daughter, I suggest you accept my offer."

He shook his head. "This isn't how I thought our conversation would go at all. I'm not sure…"

"You thought money would allow you to call the shots," I said. "Making money is great, but I choose cases based on what interests me. Perhaps we both should take some time to think about what we're getting ourselves into."

Although I meant every word of it, my insides burned. I had every intention of looking into the case of both missing girls, whether he decided to be my client or not. Mr. Tate remained silent. I assumed he was second guessing our arrangement. I took the money out of my bag and chucked it across the table. It landed half on his lap—and half on the seat he was sitting in.

He snatched the envelope and stood up. "Wait just a minute. Don't go—please."

"If I'm not the right fit for you, Mr. Tate, I understand," I said.

His shaking hand rubbed his watery eye. "Ms. Monroe,

can you imagine what it's like to lose the one you love, and just when you've given up, something happens that gives you renewed hope? I wish you could understand what it feels like."

I thought of my sister, Gabby, and the emotions I'd experienced when I learned she'd been captured and murdered by a serial killer who had no regard for human life. A serial killer who later ended up dead when he learned what happened when you messed around with the wrong girl's sister.

"You do know what it's like," he said. "I can see it in your eyes. You lost someone too, didn't you?"

"My sister."

"How then can you ask me to hand over a part of my daughter? This paper is the only connection to her existence that I have left."

I sighed. I didn't want to empathize, but I couldn't help it. But he'd still have to let go of the paper sooner or later if he expected to ever see his daughter again. Connecting the two kidnappings would reignite the flame in both cases.

"I'll make you a deal," I said. "I'll accept you as a client. But, if I find any new evidence, you agree to hand the page over without question."

He let it sink in for a moment before responding and then said, "You have my word."

"Good. I need to go home and get my things together. I'll be in touch."

He walked over, throwing his arms around me unexpectedly. "Thank you. Thank you so much. I didn't mean to be so hard on you. These last few months have been rough. Losing my daughter is hard enough, but lately it feels like I'm losing my wife too."

I leaned back, breaking from his embrace. "You have every right to be on edge right now. But I need you to remember, I'm not the enemy. I'm here to help you, and that's what I intend to do."

He nodded. I pushed the front door of the restaurant open, and we both walked out.

"Oh, one more thing," I said. "Who referred you to me?"

"Some guy I met in a bar."

"Do you remember his name?"

He scratched the side of his head. "Called himself Calhoun."

CHAPTER FIVE

Nick Calhoun. The man was, in a word, pushy. The mention of his name, or in this case, half of it, caused my anxiety to spike on several levels. I sat down in the driver's seat but didn't start the car. Instead, I opened the glove box, removing a bottle of prescription medication. I didn't take it often, but reserved it for moments of high intensity like this one.

I hadn't seen or heard from Nick in months. Not since we'd broken up over his control issues. A three-year relationship wasted—all because he couldn't meet me halfway. I even moved in with the guy when I wasn't ready, but it still wasn't enough. Nothing ever was with him. Nick had never approved of me being a private investigator, so the fact he'd mentioned me to someone else was startling.

I picked my cell phone out of my pants pocket, scanning the contact list until I spotted his name. And then I sat there, staring at Nick's number, trying to make a decision. It was time for me to experience an important rite of passage every girl endured at some point: the 'should I' or 'shouldn't I' of past relationships. I'd never met a woman who hadn't reached out to at least one of their exes, but I'd never done it. I preferred to remember why things ended and how reestablishing contact usually led to the guy getting the wrong idea about why the girl called him in the first place. Women had several different reasons for reconnecting, of course, but the main one? Closure. And I already had mine. So when I dialed his number and the phone started ringing in my ear, I was anything but prepared.

"You still with the suit?" he said.

"Hello to you too," I said.

"I didn't know how long our conversation would be, so I thought I'd get the important part out of the way at the beginning."

"You expected my call then?"

"You didn't answer my question."

"I'd rather not talk about him," I said. "He's not the reason why I called."

Nick laughed.

"So you *are* still with him? Afraid of what he'll do to you if you call it quits?"

I sighed. "Can we talk about something else?"

"Like what—the fact you refuse to speak to me?"

"The last time we spoke on the phone, you hung up," I said. "Remember?"

"There wasn't anything left to say."

"Exactly," I said.

"And now?"

Regret. And the strong urge to rewind the moment and make the decision *not* to call him at all. And an even stronger urge to purchase and consume an entire bottle of wine once I arrived back home. Or maybe two bottles.

Does every woman feel like this?

"Rusty, you still there?" he said.

"Rusty" had been Elvis's pet name for actress Ann-Margret Olsson, who supposedly considered Elvis to be the love of her life. Since Nick had felt the same way about me once upon a time, in his mind, the name applied. I never liked it. He didn't care.

"Please don't call me that," I said.

"Why not? You used to love it."

I sighed.

"Can we get back to the reason I'm calling?"

"It's still all business with you, isn't it? It was always hard trying to get you to unwind."

"What do you know, Nick?"

"Do you even think about me anymore?"

"I haven't thought about us for months."

"Why? Because you're too busy with the suit?"

"Please Nick—just stop. All I care about right now is how you know Mr. Tate."

"Fine. I was traveling through Jackson Hole last week. I was driving straight through, but I was tired, so I decided to stay the night. I went to some local bar and sat next to your guy."

"Noah Tate?"

"Obviously."

"Go on," I said.

"This Tate guy said his four-year-old daughter had been

kidnapped several months earlier. He'd come to the realization he would never see her again and had decided to kill himself and his wife."

"Wow," I said. "He left that part out of the conversation. At least he didn't do it."

"Don't get too relieved, he almost did. He said he was loading the gun when his wife came in with an envelope addressed to the two of them. He opened it and found some paper inside he claims is from his missing daughter."

"And?"

"At first I thought he was crazy. I didn't care if he was drunk or sober. I couldn't understand why he'd tell that kind of thing to someone he'd just met."

"So you thought the guy was a lunatic, and yet you gave him my card?" I said.

"I told him I'd left something in my truck and snuck away so I could check out his story. Turned out, it was true. I did a search on my phone. There were photos all over the Internet of Tate, his wife, and their missing daughter. I gave him your card because from what Tate led me to believe, he doesn't trust the police."

"Yeah, I got that impression too," I said.

"I've dealt with guys like him before—they all have the same glossed-over look in their eyes. This one's teetering on the edge. He's unpredictable, and I thought if anyone could help him, it's you."

"I don't get it," I said. "You always hated what I did for a living."

"Still do. But no matter what I think, you'll keep doing it

anyway."

"So you thought why not throw me a bone?" I said.

"Look, I genuinely question Tate's sanity. But I thought if you looked into the kidnapping, it might give him something to live for—buy the guy and his wife some time before it's too late."

CHAPTER SIX

Maddie sat on the couch with my very tired westie, Lord Berkeley, a.k.a. Boo, asleep in her lap. "Still no answer?"

"I've been calling him for three days now. The phone goes straight to voicemail every time."

Maddie squinted.

"You ever have this problem with Giovanni before?"

"Never. We've been dating for several months now, and this is the longest we've gone without talking to each other."

"Hmm. When was the last time you heard from him?"

"He called me a few days ago, saying he had some kind of urgent business to attend to in New York City. But ever since he left, I haven't heard a word—no text, no phone call, nothing. That's not a relationship. Not to me."

"Maybe he's in trouble," Maddie said.

I shook my head. "Giovanni is the type of person who starts trouble and then later ends it."

Maddie smacked me on the shoulder. "You're still hung up on the whole 'mafia' thing, aren't you?"

"It's not a 'thing,' Maddie, it's real. Just because he

refuses to talk to me about it doesn't make it any different."

"But you've never actually seen him involved in any mafia activity, so how do you know exactly what the guy does?"

"Of course I have," I said. "He just thinks I have no idea what anyone is talking about."

I stared at the lake outside my bedroom window, wishing I could climb onto my inflatable raft and fall asleep under the watchful eye of the afternoon sun.

"I'm leaving for a few days," I said.

"What—when?"

"Tomorrow morning. I took a new case yesterday."

Maddie pushed her elbows into the comforter on my bed, propping her hands onto her cheeks. Boo slid off of her and onto one of my pillows. "Where are you off to?"

"Wyoming," I said.

She laughed.

"You're joking."

"All you need is a business license."

"What's the case?"

"A kidnapping. Two kids."

She opened my nightstand drawer and rifled around.

"I don't have any gum in there," I said.

She frowned and shut the drawer. "How old are these kids?"

"The first one was six when she was kidnapped, so she'd be eight now," I said. "And the other is four."

"No wonder you took the case. How could anyone say no to a couple of missing kids?"

"The police don't have a lot of evidence from what I understand."

"How long have they been missing?"

"The older one was taken two years ago, and the younger one, six months ago."

"Mmmph," Maddie said. "I don't like those odds. You know you have almost no chance of finding them alive."

"I know, but I have to at least try," I said. "One piece of evidence has been nagging at me. Both parents received a coloring page in the mail leading them to believe it came from their child."

Maddie made a face like she'd just bit into something sour. "What a cruel thing to do."

"I don't know what to make of it yet, but my client is convinced the coloring page was drawn by his daughter."

"Why would someone take a person's child and then send them reminders of it? Was there a ransom?"

I shook my head.

"There's been no other contact with the parents of either child other than the one coloring page they each received in the mail," I said. "I've been going over it all day, trying to figure out why a person with no ulterior motive would take the time to send it at all."

"And what did you come up with?"

"There's only one motive that comes to mind: guilt."

CHAPTER SEVEN

Instead of calling Giovanni again the next morning, I tried my luck with his right-hand man, Lucio. He answered on the second ring.

"Hey, Sloane."

"I need to talk to Giovanni," I said. "I've been calling for a few days."

"Boss can't talk right now. He's in an important meetin'. Said to tell you he should be home soon."

"That's it?"

"Oh and uh, one more thing—he said not to worry. He'll explain everything later."

"He's too busy to send a text?" I said. "It's been four days, Lucio. What's going on?"

"Don't get all bent, Sloane."

"I'm not," I said.

"Sure sounds like it. Things here are, ahh, complicated at the moment."

How complicated could they possibly be?

I sat there trying to decide whether it was worth saying

something I might regret later. It probably was, but I stayed quiet.

"Sloane, you still there?"

"I'm here," I said.

"Want me to give the boss a message for you?"

"Yes. Tell him I won't be around when he gets back in town."

"Why? Where you goin'?"

"Just tell Giovanni not to worry, okay?" I said. "If he can explain everything later, so can I."

I pressed the end button on my cell phone and sent it to voicemail when Lucio called back. I zipped my suitcase closed and looked around for Lord Berkeley who'd been MIA for the last half hour. The dog had good instincts. He knew whenever I put my shoes on, I was leaving. Combine that with packing a bag, it usually meant he was going to a sitter for a few days, something he didn't particularly like.

I called Lord Berkeley's name out several times, but the only response I got was a room full of silence. There was only one thing to do. I walked to my front door, opened it, and knocked. Boo scampered around the corner in full alert mode, teeth clenched, growling at the door. It worked every time.

"Let's go for a ride," I said.

He gave me a look that said, Listen lady, I know what the word 'ride' means. And I'm not going to no sitter.

"It's okay," I said. "You can come with me this time."

He didn't understand, but when he spotted the bag of dog treats I rattled around in my hand, it no longer mattered.

I heard a noise behind me that sounded like someone roller blading on the pavement. I turned around, facing the blond, pigtailed woman in front of me.

"All ready to go," Maddie said.

"Umm, what are you talking about?"

She smacked me on the arm. "I'm your plus one."

"I already have a 'plus one,'" I said, pointing at Lord Berkeley.

"Oh, come on. You're such a stiff sometimes," she said. "I need a vacation, and you're going somewhere I haven't been before, so I figured I'd tag along and keep you company. Besides, if I don't go, you'll just call me with a bunch of questions anyway. You always do."

I walked past her.

"I'm going whether you like it or not," Maddie said.

I turned, looking her in the eye.

"I'm looking for missing children this time, not dead bodies. At least, I am hoping it won't come to that."

"Just because you *think* you're better on your own, doesn't mean you are. How many people in your line of work can say they have a medical examiner at their disposal?"

"Will it matter if I say no?" I said.

Maddie smiled, knowing she'd won. Not many people did with me. "You don't have anything to worry about. I'll stay out of your way."

I glanced at the cut-off denim shorts and pointy boots she was wearing and somehow didn't believe a word of it. "What's with the outfit?"

"You said Wyoming, right?"

"Yeah—but not Wyoming streetwalker."

She tossed her head back and laughed.

"I bet half the girls in the state dress like this. You'll see."

Four hours and one pit stop later, we pulled into a three-star hotel on the outskirts of town.

Maddie stuck her bottom lip out like a child who'd just been told there wouldn't be any dessert tonight. "Where are we?"

"Pinedale," I said.

"I thought we were going to Jackson Hole?"

"We are, but I want to look around here first."

"Why?"

"This is where the first kidnapping took place," I said.

"But the guy who hired you was from the second kidnapping, right?"

I nodded.

"Going to Jackson right now would be like crossing the finish line before starting the race," I said. "I need to start at the beginning, where it all happened."

She wasn't listening anymore. Her attention had been diverted to the exterior of the hotel. She waved her hand in front of her. "This is the best you could do?"

"What's wrong with it?" I said.

"I'm in charge of making the reservations from now on."

I shrugged.

"I'm not sure they have five-star hotels in this town. You might be on vacation, I'm not. Five-hundred-thread-count sheets won't help me find two lost girls."

She smiled.

"Yeah, but getting good sleep might."

I glanced at the time on my phone. "I need to run into town really quick."

"Can't it wait until morning?"

I shook my head.

"I want to stop by the grocery store before they close." I snapped Boo's leash on his collar and handed it to her. "There's a pool. And a Jacuzzi. You'll be fine."

A black Dodge Ram circled the parking lot and then exited without stopping. Normally, it would have flown under my radar, but the black grille guard on the front caught my eye. I'd seen a similar truck before in the McDonald's parking lot the day before when I met with Noah Tate. But the Dodge hadn't even slowed as it passed by, and there was no reason for me to believe I was being followed. Not yet. I shook it off. After all, I was in Wyoming where trucks were a dime a dozen. Right?

CHAPTER EIGHT

The lights inside Maybelle's Market were still on when I arrived, and according to the sign in the window, I had twenty minutes before they closed. I was determined to make the most of it.

A young girl about the age of eighteen was politely giving instructions to a coworker when I walked in. She wore a red apron with the store's name embroidered on the front. When I walked by, she looked at me and smiled, showcasing a mouth full of perfectly positioned porcelain veneers. They reminded me of white Chicklet's gum and were so bright I couldn't look away no matter how hard I tried.

"Can I help you?" she said.

"Is the manager here?"

She thumbed to the right. "He's in his office. Is everything all right?"

I nodded.

"I just wanted to ask him a few questions."

"I can get him for you if you want."

"How long have you worked here?" I said.

She paused for so long I thought I was going to be given the actual date and time right down to the last second.

"I kinda grew up here. My dad owns the store."

"So you're a Maybelle?"

Her laugh made me feel like I'd missed out on an inside joke. "Maybelle's isn't our last name. The store was named after Myra Maybelle Shirley, a famous outlaw. They used to call her "The Bandit Queen." When my grandpa first opened the store, all he sold was coffee and that type of thing. He passed the store down to my dad, and now we sell practically everything."

A man stepped out of a side office, a set of keys swinging from his pointer finger. He glanced at me and then checked the time on his wristwatch. Obviously, he had one thing on his mind: closing the store. He wore a faded white polo shirt that was several sizes too big and a pair of slacks that couldn't hold their position without a belt. The man walked past us and then stopped. "Is there a problem?"

I shook my head.

"This young lady was just telling me about the history of this place."

He shooed the girl away with his hand and came closer. "Do you need help finding something? We're closing in five minutes."

"I believe I've found what I was looking for," I said.

His eyes searched my empty hands.

"Is there somewhere we can talk for a minute?" I said.

"What about?"

"Olivia Hathaway."

The man whipped around and speed-walked so fast back into his office I could barely keep up with him. He held the door, ushering me into his office. Once inside, he closed the door, leaning against it like it was a welcome refuge from potential eavesdroppers on the outside.

His office smelled like a combination of an old jock strap and stale food, prompting me to keep our meeting short.

"Is there a problem?" I said.

"Who are you?"

"Not a reporter if that's what you're worried about," I said.

"I've never seen you before, and you don't look like you're from here."

I glanced down at my jeans and lavender sweater, wondering what he would have thought if I'd brought Maddie along with me. But he wasn't eyeing my clothes. He was scrutinizing my Fendi handbag, a gift from Giovanni. I considered setting the major distraction on the floor until I noticed it looked like it hadn't been mopped for a while. Apparently, store cleanliness didn't extend to personal offices. I held the bag securely with both hands in front of me, tight against my legs to avoid contamination.

"My name is Sloane," I said.

"Jim."

Jim sat behind a beaten up metal desk that quite possibly had been around since his father owned the store. I sat opposite him on a chair that had a price tag dangling from the side. At least it was clean.

"I'm looking into the kidnapping of a couple girls over

the past two years," I said.   "I understand Olivia was kidnapped from your store."

He cleared his throat—twice. "I told everything I know to the cops, and then to the investigators that showed up after the cops, and then to the agents who showed up after the investigators. Why are you interested?"

"I've been hired to look into a few things."

"Are you new?"

"New?" I said.

"Did they bring you in because the last two guys didn't find anything?"

I shook my head.

"I'm not a cop."

"Then what are you?"

"A private investigator."

His eyes widened as if shocked people like me actually existed. "You shittin' me? Olivia's parents don't got much money, so who hired you?"

"I can't say."

He leaned forward, resting his elbows on the desk. "Can't or won't?"

I smiled.

"It's the same thing, isn't it?"

I'd smarted off, maybe a little too much for Jim's liking, but his body language had already told me that while the store was open, he was closed.

"I'd better not talk to you."

"All I want to know is what happened the day Olivia was taken," I said.

"It was in the paper. Look it up."

"I have," I said. "I'm interested in hearing about your side of things."

"It's no different."

"So there's nothing you didn't tell police—not one detail you left out?"

He raised a brow.

"Are you calling me a liar?"

"I haven't called you anything," I said.

Yet.

He stood, hovering over me with his arms spread out over both sides of the desk like he expected it to produce a dramatic and lasting effect. But he wasn't the first bully I'd gone up against, and he wouldn't be the last.

"I want you to leave," he said. "And don't bother my daughter on the way out. People in this town are protective of each other. They won't take kindly to you poking your nose around where it don't belong. I'd move on if I were you."

I left the store like he asked, but when I got in the car and shut the door, it miraculously opened back up again. Jim's daughter and her teeth stood in the doorway. She glanced around the parking lot and hunched over.

"My name's Jenny, by the way."

Jim and Jenny. I wondered if all the names in their family started with a "J."

"Sloane," I said.

"I'm sorry I opened your door without permission. It's just—I overheard you talking to my dad."

"How?" I said. "The office door was shut."

"The air vents in my dad's office are connected to the ones in the next room, and well, I didn't mean to eavesdrop—"

"But you did," I said.

"There's someone you should talk to while you're in town."

"Who?"

"His name is Todd Anderson. The day Olivia was kidnapped, he was here."

"Working?"

She nodded.

"We were dating at the time. At least, we were trying to, but then my dad found out."

"He didn't approve?" I said.

She shook her head no.

"Why not?" I said.

She poked her head over the roof of my car, looked around, and then ducked down again. "Todd was in a band, only it wasn't even a band, really. I tried to tell my dad that, but he didn't care. He fired Todd to keep him from seeing me."

"That doesn't seem fair."

"It wasn't."

"Why do I need to talk to him?" I said.

"Because on the day Olivia was kidnapped, he saw something."

CHAPTER NINE

Maddie and I sat in a car across the street from Todd's house the next morning. A group of misfit boys belted out a "pitchy" tune in an open garage with an oversized piece of green and orange shag carpeting on the floor. From where we sat, I couldn't determine what type of music it was exactly, but it sounded like the yelling kind.

When I had spoken to Jenny the night before, she admitted she'd tried to get Todd to tell her what he saw the day Olivia was abducted. But every time she brought it up, he acted weird about it, always changing the subject. I asked her why she didn't say something about it to her father, or the police. Her answer was simple: she said she wouldn't tell. And since Todd hadn't elaborated on what he saw that day, Jenny wasn't sure how much it mattered. I couldn't understand why she kept something so important to herself, but then again, she was young. Maybe at her age she couldn't comprehend how a simple piece of information could make such a big difference.

"So which one do you think he is?" Maddie said.

I opened the car door. "Let's find out."

By the time we were halfway across the street, the music had stopped, and all eyes were on Maddie who was showing more skin than clothing. She hadn't bothered to change after her dip in the pool earlier that morning, and had just thrown a cover-up over her bikini, announcing she was "ready to go." The only problem was, I couldn't figure out what the cover-up "covered up;" the sheer fabric showed everything. She didn't seem to care. The boys didn't either.

One of the boys set his guitar to the side and walked down the driveway to greet us. "Can I help you, ladies?"

"Which one of you is Todd?" I said.

Inside the garage, a boy with brown, shaggy, moppish-looking hair and small silver hoop earrings raised a single finger into the air.

A boy standing next to Todd socked him in the shoulder. "He's Todd. And I'm John. Oh, and that's Paul," he said pointing at the boy in front of us.

Maddie laughed. "Where's Ringo?"

Unfortunately, Maddie and I were the only ones old enough to get the joke.

Todd, a.k.a. lead singer of screaming boy band, eyeballed me with curiosity but didn't say a word.

"Now that I know who everyone is, I need to talk to Todd for a minute," I said.

"What for?" Todd said.

The boy standing next to Todd gave him a look like he was crazy. "Dude, why does it matter?"

"You used to work at Maybelle's, right?" I said.

Todd shrugged.

"With Jenny? She's quite fond of you. She wanted me to say hello."

"What are you, like, a relative of hers or something?" Todd said.

Maddie beamed with pride, blurting out, "She's a private investigator."

She and I exchanged the kind of look only a friend would understand, and although I was confident there would be no further outbursts, it was too late; all three of the boys looked at each other like they'd just been caught skinny dipping in the principal's pool.

The boy standing in front of us fidgeted with a pick he held in his hand, flipping it over and over until it got to the point I thought he'd worn down the skin under one of his fingers. "Is this about the other night, 'cause we already told the cops, it wasn't our weed. We were just—"

"Relax," I said. "Cops don't send private investigators out over a bag of weed."

"Why you here then?" Todd said. "I haven't seen Jenny since her dad fired me."

"I wanted to ask you about Olivia."

"Who?" Todd said.

The boy standing next to Todd socked him—again. "Don't you remember? The missing chick."

I appreciated teenagers who didn't know how to keep their mouths shut.

The realization hit Todd like Evander Holyfield the moment he realized Mike Tyson had, in fact, taken a bite out of crime.

In the midst of all this, Maddie entered the garage, sitting down behind a set of drums. With a drumstick in each hand, she looked at Todd and said, "You," tap-tap "saw" tap-tap "something."

I glanced at Todd, finishing the jingle. "And I'm here to find out what."

Todd glanced at the door of the house like he wished he was behind it.

"I'm not here to get you in trouble," I said. "I just need some information. Then I'll leave, and you won't see me again."

Todd looked at his friends and then at the ground. "I—I don't wanna talk about it."

I faced Maddie, giving her the *I-need-to-get-him-alone* look.

She pointed her drumsticks at John and Paul. "So, boys—which one of you wants to show me how to really play this thing?"

They stepped up to the plate simultaneously. Todd walked into the house. I followed. Thankfully, no parents were in sight. It appeared to be a bachelor pad.

It took a moment for Todd to notice I was still in tow, but when he finally glanced back, he muttered something to himself and then shook his head. "You can't just walk into my house," he said without turning around.

I smiled.

"I just did," I said.

"Get out."

"No."

"Get out or I'll—"

"Go ahead," I said. "Call the police. Then we can all hear about the secret you've been keeping."

Todd rounded the corner and looked at me. His face had paled, turning a dull, ashen color. He leaned against the living room wall and then slid toward the ground like he was melting. He probably felt like he was. When his butt hit the carpeted floor, he crossed his arms over his knees, burying his head as far as it would go between them.

I walked over and knelt down in front of him. "Is it really that bad? I'm not here to judge you. Whatever it is, you can tell me."

His silence was a challenge, but not the hardest one I'd ever faced. He just needed a little encouragement.

"About six months ago, a toddler named Savannah Tate was kidnapped from a daycare in Jackson Hole," I said. "And do you want to know something? She was only four years old. Olivia was six when she was taken, but you already know that. You were there that day."

I waited a full minute, but he didn't budge, and with his head buried in what he must have wished was sand, I couldn't tell whether my words had any effect on him. All I could do was to keep talking until I struck a chord.

"When things like this happen, it's not only the child who suffers, their parents do too. I've met Savannah's father. He's heartbroken, and her mother can't even get out of bed. They've been so distraught over losing their daughter, neither one of them cares if they live or die. It's hard enough for a parent to lose a child, but to take their own life—I can't imagine what that kind of grief must feel like."

His breathing quickened, and for a moment, I worried he'd hyperventilate. Then it slowed again, but he still wasn't coming around.

"Do you want to know what I think?" I said. "I think the same kidnapper took both Olivia and Savannah. But in order to prove it, I need you to tell me what you saw. Will you help me?"

Todd lifted his head just enough to give me the hope I was looking for. "The girl you were just talking about—"

"Savannah?"

He nodded.

"Her parents—they didn't kill themselves, did they?"

At last.

"Savannah's father had the gun loaded with two bullets in the clip: one for his wife, the other for him."

"But he didn't go through with it, right?"

"Not yet," I said. "But if I can't help him find out what happened to his daughter, I'm afraid they might not make it next time."

Todd sighed, looking away for a brief moment. Then he shifted his focus back to the carpet again. "If I tell you what I saw, I'll get in trouble."

"With who—the police?"

He nodded.

"I read about it—it's called withholding evidence."

"I'll do everything I can to make sure that doesn't happen," I said.

He paused. I waited.

"I may have seen Olivia."

"You 'may have' or you did?" I said.

"I saw her," he said.

"Where? Did you see the person who was with her?"

His bottom lip trembled. "I saw them both in the parking lot. I watched the man take her. I watched him, and I didn't do anything about it."

CHAPTER TEN

Todd was sobbing, his tears dripping into his hands as he tried to sweep them out of his face. I wanted to give him time to recover before he revealed what he'd kept bottled up for the past two years, but with a couple teenagers outside being watched over by a less-than-competent babysitter, I couldn't wait long.

"I know how hard it must be to relive what happened," I said, "but I need to know what you saw."

He glared at me like I was hard of hearing. "I just told you."

"You haven't given me anything I can use."

Not yet.

I went to the kitchen, poured a glass of water, and handed it out to him. "Here."

He waved it away. "I don't want it."

"You need it," I said.

I held it out until he took it from my hand. He gulped it down in a matter of seconds.

"You said you watched the man take her. Didn't the

police question you or ask where you were when Olivia was taken?"

He nodded.

"I told them I didn't see anything."

He'd lied. Great. It seemed like the withholding-information virus was going around lately.

"Well, now I know that you did," I said, "and I need all the details."

He shrugged.

"Like what?"

"Pretend I'm someone who has never heard the story before," I said. "How would you explain it to me?"

Todd looked up and to the right, an indicator that he was piecing together the visual images he remembered from the day of Olivia's abduction.

"Let's start with this," I said. "Tell me what you were doing when you first saw Olivia."

He nodded.

"I'd just finished helping a woman load some grocery bags in her trunk. After she left, I scanned the parking lot for shopping carts, loaded some up, and was getting ready to take them in. A grocery ad fell out of one of the carts. I bent down to pick it up, and that's when I saw the little girl."

"What was she doing?" I said.

"Walking. A man was holding her hand. At first I thought the guy was her dad because he kept smiling down at her, but she looked scared. She wouldn't even look at him."

"Describe the man to me."

Todd shrugged.

"Tall."

"How tall?" I said.

"Maybe a few inches taller than me."

"You're tall. Are you saying the man was around six foot six?"

"Guess so."

"What else did you notice?"

"He wore a hat."

"What kind?"

"A ball cap."

"Color?"

"Red."

"Did the ball cap have anything on it—was it for a sports team, maybe?"

"I don't remember. I don't think so. He had on a pair of mirrored sunglasses. You know, the kind you can see yourself in."

"What about his clothes?" I said.

"Black T-shirt and jeans."

"Shoes?"

"I don't remember."

"What was his hair like?" I said.

"Average, I guess."

I tried again.

"Was it long or short? How much of it was coming out of the ball cap?"

"I couldn't tell."

"Did he see you?" I said.

Todd shook his head.

"He was too busy talking to some old lady who'd followed him to his car."

"What did the car look like?"

"It was silver."

"What about a make and model?" I said.

"It was a Dodge Charger, I think. It had dark, tinted windows. I couldn't see inside from where I was squatting."

First Mr. Tate refuses to turn over the coloring page and now this. *What was wrong with these people?* Part of me had an urge to slap Todd across the face. The information he had would have given police a strong lead, one that could have saved a little girl's life. Todd may have been a teenager, but he was also a coward.

I needed to keep going; I wasn't finished with him yet.

"What happened between the man and the lady who stopped him?" I said.

"The lady said something to him, but he didn't even look at her, he just kept walking."

"Then what?"

"The man opened the back door of his car, put the little girl inside, and when he turned around he saw the lady was standing behind him. He said something to her and then the lady fell down. At first I thought it was an accident, but then the man didn't bend down to help her."

"What did you do?" I said.

"I—"

His voice was shaky.

"Tell me. It's okay."

He shook his head.

"No. It isn't. I could have done something, but I didn't. I just stayed there, crouched on the ground while he ran over the old lady's body. I was confused. It happened so fast. When I went back into the store, I heard Olivia's mother calling for her, and that's when I knew what was really going on."

I was too upset to say anything, which I was sure Todd gathered when he looked at my face.

"Don't you understand? If they found out I was outside, they would have wanted to know why I didn't do anything to stop the man from taking her. Everyone in town would have known."

"You are the only witness, Todd. Don't you think everyone would have been grateful to you for telling the truth?"

He shrugged.

"It's too late now. They'll all hate me for it."

I placed my hand on his shoulder. "Aren't you tired of carrying this around? Don't you want to help Olivia's parents? What if there's a chance their daughter is still alive?"

He looked scared. "What are you saying?"

"Telling me isn't the same thing as telling the authorities," I said. "I'm glad you finally did the right thing, but they need to know everything. You *have* to tell them."

"I can't do it—I won't! You know what happened now. Isn't that enough?"

"It isn't," I said. I walked to the door, turning around slightly before opening it. "You've got twenty-four hours to talk to the police. After that, I'll tell them where to find you. And do everyone a favor, don't run. Then I'll have to track you down, and I don't have time for it right now."

He tapped his Converse shoe on the ground. "This isn't fair. You tricked me! I lied to the police. I could go to jail."

"Olivia may have lost her life because of your silence. You need to make things right."

CHAPTER ELEVEN

I dropped Maddie off at the hotel and unfolded a map of the town, spreading it out over the steering wheel in front of me. In months past, I'd thought about getting a GPS, or even using the map application I had on my iPhone. But ever since my grandfather had taught me how to use a printed map, I'd never been led astray. Besides, what people said about old habits was true—and most of mine were alive and well.

One sixty-eight Pinecone Avenue was the easiest house on the street to locate given the large green ribbons wrapped around a cluster of pine trees in the corner of the front yard. At the base of the trees photos, candles, and even a few weathered and worn teddy bears stood as a reminder that Olivia may have been gone, but she was not forgotten.

The shrine in Olivia's yard reminded me of a trip I'd taken to Ground Zero a few months after nine eleven. Maybe I should have been scared to fly there, with the nation on high alert and all, but I wasn't. I'd been afraid of few things in my life, and dying wasn't one of them. The chain-link fence surrounding the area where the twin towers had once stood offered visitors a view of heaping dirt piles and broken concrete. The fence, an attraction of its own, had been covered with everything from flowers to poems written by compassionate people from all walks of life. But that wasn't what I'd noticed most. It was the silence. The eerie, chilling silence—the kind of quiet hush that makes a person feel like they're not alone in a room, even when they are.

"Can I help you?" said a female voice from behind me.

I turned to see a woman in a yellow dress. A knitted shawl was wrapped around her arms. The wrinkles around her eyes gave the appearance of someone much older than me, even though I guessed she was young enough to be my own daughter. Almost.

"Hello," I said. "You must be Olivia's mother."

She nodded.

"My name is Kris. Who are you?"

Across the street I could see an older woman peeking at us through a lifted slat in her mini blinds. I imagined she thought I hadn't noticed, but the constant bobbing up and down of the two-inch slat was a clear indicator we were being watched. And I guessed she wasn't the only one watching.

"I wondered if I could talk to you for a few minutes about your daughter," I said, turning back to Kris.

"Are you a—"

"Reporter or a cop? No."

"Then who are you?"

Kris's next-door neighbor turned on the outside water, grabbed the hose, and started watering a patch of flowers right next to the spot Kris and I were standing. I wondered if the neighbor realized how odd she looked sprinkling water onto flowers that looked like no amount of resuscitation could ever bring them back to life. It was obvious they hadn't seen a drop of moisture in weeks. This didn't seem to deter the woman who stared down at the crop like she expected a full recovery at any moment.

Kris smiled at her neighbor, but it was one of those strained half-smiles, the kind one woman gives to another woman they're trying to avoid.

"How are you today, Sylvia?" Kris said to her neighbor.

Sylvia glanced over, shocked to see us standing there. "I'm well. Who's your friend?"

I couldn't help myself.

"Kris and I went to high school together," I said. "I was passing through town and thought I'd stop by and see what she's been up to lately." I looked at Kris. "Why don't we go inside?"

Once the door was closed, Kris said, "I don't know how I feel about you lying to my neighbor. I don't even know you."

"It doesn't take much to understand the women on this street have nothing better to do with their lives than to keep their nose in yours." I stuck my hand out. "My name is Sloane Monroe. I'm a private investigator hired by Noah Tate. I believe you know him?"

Kris stood there looking at my hand, stunned by my revelation.

"It's okay. He told me he talked to you. And I know about what he received in the mail."

Kris walked to the sofa and sat down.

"So you are—looking for his daughter?" she said. "He said he was going to hire someone before taking the paper to the police. To be honest, I didn't believe him."

"I am looking for his daughter. And yours."

"Mine? I don't know what he told you, but if you've come here for money, I can't—"

"I'm not here for money," I said. "I just want to ask you a few questions."

"Why do you want to help me?"

"There's a good chance we're dealing with the same kidnapper."

"You know, I told Mr. Tate he needed to keep working with the police. I've been conflicted about whether or not to tell the authorities myself—it would help them find both our daughters, don't you think?"

"I do," I said. "I'll be meeting with him in the next day or two, and I'll be sure the detective who's working on the case is apprised of the recent development. You have nothing to worry about."

Kris seemed relieved. "How can I help you?"

I spent the next few minutes asking her the same questions she'd probably heard a thousand times before. The answers rolled off her tongue, requiring little to no thought. I wanted to tell her about Todd, but I hesitated. The truth would come out soon enough.

Although two years had passed, it had taken a noticeable toll on her. Her voice was soft, so much so that I had to ask her to repeat herself a few times. Kris was running on fumes, tired and worn out while the search persevered. She said she wrote a letter to Olivia every day, even though she didn't know if she'd ever see her again. If she ever did, Kris wanted to make sure her daughter heard all the things she might have missed.

When Kris finished, I asked her if I could take a look at Olivia's room. She rubbed the top of her fingernail so hard with the edge of her thumbnail; I thought she'd scratch the polish off.

"Is there something wrong?" I said. "If it makes you uncomfortable, you don't have to show it to me."

"It's just—her room doesn't look like it used to, before the, well before." She stood up. "Let me show you."

I followed Kris to the bedroom expecting to find the things one normally does in a child's room, but what I saw alarmed me. It looked a lot more like a hunting storage room than anything else. "This was Olivia's room?"

From the looks of things, someone must have decided Olivia wasn't coming back.

"Olivia's dad has a lot of hunting stuff," I said.

"Step-dad."

"For how long?"

"Terrence and I married when Olivia was five, a year before she was taken."

"But you and Olivia share the same last name," I said.

She nodded.

"I didn't take on Terrence's last name when I married. I thought it would be confusing for Olivia, and he didn't seem to mind."

"What was their relationship like?"

She shrugged.

"It was all right."

Her voice said all right, but her face said something else.

"So they got along?" I said.

"Olivia's biological father never had much to do with her. It was hard on Terrence at first. He's never had any children. But he tolerated her. They got along."

Tolerated her? She was a child, not a dog.

"So the last name Hathaway. Is that—"

"My maiden name."

"When did Terrence decide to turn Olivia's room into a man cave?" I said.

"We didn't have much room and—it wasn't my idea. I wanted to keep it the same, just the way she left it."

"And Terrence didn't agree with you?"

"He said Olivia wasn't coming back, and at some point, I had to accept it and move on. I guess this is his way of helping me."

What a cold-blooded way to "help" someone.

"Where does Olivia's father live now—her real one?"

Kris teared up for a moment, but then regained her composure. "I don't know."

"You said he wasn't in her life much, but did she ever see him?" I said. "Are you sure he didn't have anything to do with her disappearance?"

"That's not possible."

"But you just said you don't know where he is. Have the police tried to find him?"

She shook her head.

"Why not?" I said.

"I don't know where he is because I don't know who he is."

Kris braced her hand against the wall, steadying herself.

"Do you need to sit down?" I said.

She nodded. We returned to the living room.

"It was spring break," she said. "I was in California with several of my girlfriends. It was crazy. I hung out with a few different guys while I was there, but I never knew any of their last names, only their first. A couple months after, I found out I was pregnant with Olivia."

"I imagine you were shocked," I said.

"I have a lot of regrets in my life, but Olivia wasn't one of them."

"How did your family react to the news?"

"My dad was upset at first, but once he got used to the idea, both of my parents were supportive. I lived with them until I met Terrence. I didn't think anyone would marry me since I'd had a child under those circumstances, but then Terrence came along. He said he would marry me, but he didn't want any kids. Of course, I already had Olivia, so he said that was fine, as long as we didn't have any children together."

"What about you—did you want more kids?" I said.

"When I was younger, I thought I'd have several kids. But at least I had one."

"Did Terrence know how you felt?"

"I tried talking to him once. All he said was, 'we made a

deal.'"

A picture was forming in my mind of the type of guy Terrence was—it wasn't pleasant. I didn't know how she didn't see it. But women with Kris's meek personality rarely did. She talked about him like he was some kind of super-hero who showed up when she needed rescuing.

I asked Kris a few more questions, but learned nothing I didn't already know. I stood up to leave, promising to get in touch with her if I found out anything new. Outside a black Dodge Ram drove by. It looked just like the one I'd seen in Evanston and then again at my hotel. The next time I saw it, I'd be ready.

CHAPTER TWELVE

"Pssst, over here," a voice called from the bushes.

I had exited Kris's home and was on my way to my car when I heard it. I walked "over here" and came face to face with Sylvia and another woman I guessed to be the one staring through the blinds. They were revved up but doe-eyed at the same time. Something pressing was on their minds—I could tell by their rapid breathing. It was fast and intense, like the words they had prepared to say were getting ready to explode all over everything.

"What can I do for you two?" I said.

Sylvia wagged her finger at me. "We know you didn't go to school with Kris."

"Yeah, we've known Kris since she was this tall," Mini-Blind Lady gestured with her outstretched, flattened hand.

"What I'm doing here doesn't concern either of you, and it's not polite to linger outside Kris's home."

They looked at each other, contemplating their next move.

"Are you a cop or something?" Sylvia said. "Because

we've seen everyone who's come in and out of this place, but we've never seen you before."

I nodded.   I may not have been a cop, but I had no problem putting myself into the "or something" category.

Sylvia elbowed her friend. "See, Mildred, I told you." She then looked at me. "If you're looking into what happened to Olivia, you'll want to hear what we have to say."

I pointed to my car. "Get in."

They exchanged looks again.

"Look," I said, "whatever it is, I'm not going to discuss it here. We can go to the end of the street and talk there. And if you two don't trust me, fine. But I'm leaving."

One minute later we were parked in front of a vacant lot on the next street. Sylvia spoke up first. "That evil man killed our Judith."

"You mean Olivia?"

It seemed entirely possible that at least one of them was battling Alzheimer's.

Sylvia shook her head.

"I mean Judith Schroeder."

"The woman the kidnapper ran over in the Maybelle's Market parking lot?"

Both women nodded in unison.

"Do you know something about the kidnapping?"

Their smiles told me they did, or they thought they did.

"We know who did it," Sylvia said, eyes glimmering.

"Who?"

"Terrence."

"Olivia's stepdad?"

"Oh, we don't believe Terrence did it himself," Sylvia said.

"No, no. He wouldn't do that," Mildred said. "We think he hired someone."

"To do what?"

"Get rid of the girl, of course," Sylvia said.

Things were starting to get interesting.

"Terrence hated Olivia," Sylvia said.

"How do you know?"

"Well—" Sylvia said, "I was picking some tomatoes in my garden one evening, and I overheard Terrence tell Kris that he'd never agreed to raise Olivia, and if she wouldn't send the child to live with her parents, he was leaving."

"What did Kris say?"

"She didn't say anything," Sylvia said, "unless it was under her breath."

Mildred looked at Sylvia. "It's possible."

"Entirely," Sylvia replied. "I hadn't thought of that. My hearing isn't what it used to be. Still, I believe I would have at least heard Kris if she'd said something."

The problem with their theory was the connection to the second missing child; there was none. Not that I knew of, anyway. I started to think they'd been watching too many episodes of 48 Hours. But a lead was a lead, nonetheless.

"Have you spoken to anyone about this?" I said.

Sylvia nodded. "Oh yes. Detective Whittaker. He's been trying to find out what happened to Olivia since the day she disappeared. He's a good man."

Mildred blushed when Sylvia mentioned his name.

"What did the detective say?"

"Nothing," Sylvia said.

"Not one word?"

"Now that I think of it, Sylvia, he did say one thing," Mildred said. "He said, 'I see.'"

"And we've been waiting to hear back from him ever since," Sylvia said.

'I see' was the polite way of letting them know he didn't take anything they said seriously. So...should I?

Kris had a look of bewilderment on her face when I arrived on her doorstep for the second time in one hour.

"I have a few more questions about Terrence," I said.

Her left eye twitched, and she crossed one arm over the other in front of her. She'd been through so much already. I thought about phrasing my questions so they didn't sound so direct and invasive, but tact didn't make the top-ten list of my most admirable qualities. Hell, it didn't even make the top twenty.

"You said Terrence was fine with Olivia as long as the two of you didn't have any more children," I said. "At any time did he try to get you to get rid of her?"

The look on Kris's face answered the question for me. "What do you mean?"

"Did Terrence ever suggest that Olivia go to your parents' house to be raised by them instead of you?" I said.

"Who told you that?"

"You said he was tolerant of her," I said, "but from what I understand, it sounds like he wanted to pawn her off so the two of you could be together with no distractions."

"It's hard enough to grieve, but to be put through the same questions over and over again until you have the answers memorized. It's too much."

Kris stepped back, slowly closing the door on my question and me. I allowed it. The pain in her eyes kept me from probing any further.

"I can't do this anymore," she whispered. "I'm sorry. I just can't."

CHAPTER THIRTEEN

Thanks to Sylvia and Company, I learned Terrence worked as a night manager at a fancy restaurant inside a resort-type place by the lake. A row of a dozen or so cabins lined the left side of the street, with the lodge sitting majestically on the right. The accommodations were far superior to the hotel I was currently in, making me glad Maddie wasn't with me.

I stood at the lake's edge, taking in the glassy stillness of the water's surface. It didn't take long for my mind to wander to a place where others' didn't. A quiet, unsuspecting lake, the perfect place for a murder. I imagined two young girls hogtied and weighted down, maybe with a piece of hardened concrete, or maybe to a cluster of rocks that had been secured inside a netted bag. After the restaurant closed and the resident visitors were asleep in their beds, a man would paddle the girls to the center of the lake. He wouldn't worry about them making noise, because he knew they were too terrified to cry. Once he reached the deepest part of the lake, he'd tell the girls to stand, and after they did, he'd shove them both from behind, watching their bodies sink into the cold darkness below.

I blinked back to reality, wondering why I couldn't see what everyone else did—it was a lake, just a simple, innocent body of water. What was wrong with me?

Outside the restaurant, a couple sat across from each other at a table on the veranda, holding hands and staring into one another's eyes like they were the only two people in existence. They reeked of young love, and for a moment I felt a smidgen of jealousy. Just a bit. Nothing more. After a moment the feeling was gone. I pushed open the door to the restaurant and walked inside.

It didn't take long to locate Terrence. He was the only one not dressed in a white long-sleeved shirt with pea-sized black buttons. He was older than I thought he'd be, possibly in his late thirties, or early forties, and he had a silly-looking mustache that curled slightly upward at the ends. It was very Doc Holliday-esque, but this wasn't Tombstone, and Terrence was no Val Kilmer. Not even close.

Terrence glanced in my direction, just before the scene unfolding behind me demanded his attention. I turned, expecting to see a young woman in an ill-fitted dress, but noticed an overturned glass of beer instead, and two men too liquored up to notice. The men laughed while the contents of the beer continued to gush onto the floor, narrowly missing an older woman's nylon stocking at the next table over. The woman threw down her napkin, expressing her disdain to the man sitting next to her. Just as her companion was about to stand, Terrence brushed past me, his shoulder pushing me aside in the process.

"Buck, it's time for you and Hal to go," Terrence said. "I'll call you a cab."

Terrence snapped his fingers, and a woman appeared, towel in hand.

One of the men attempted to stand. He rested his hand on Terrence's shoulder, pausing for a moment to look at the now empty glass of beer like he wasn't sure how it got that way. "Aww, hell, Terrence—it was an accident. Give me the cloth; I'll clean it for ya."

Terrence looked at the girl holding the towel. "Call a cab for these two gentlemen, then clean this table off."

She acknowledged him with a nod, turned, and went.

Some time passed before the men relented, finally realizing they couldn't talk their way out of this one. Once they were secured inside a cab, Terrence turned his attention to me. "I'm sorry. Show's over."

"Good thing it wasn't what I was here for then," I said.

"Did you need something?"

"When do you get off?" I said.

"Ma'am, I'm married."

"And I'm not interested."

He raised a brow.

"Oh, I thought—"

"Wrong."

He leaned against the counter as if he was trying to discover what I was after.

"Now I feel like a horse's ass. Can I get you anything?"

I nodded.

"Your time," I said. "Ten minutes if you can spare it."

His confusion amplified, but keeping him in suspense was getting me somewhere, so I stuck with it.

"I don't get off for another forty-five minutes."

"No problem," I said. "I'll wait."

Terrence met me in the parking lot an hour later.

"What's this all about?"

"Olivia," I said.

He rolled his eyes so far back into his head I wasn't sure whether they'd make it back out. "Figures."

"Is that why you didn't press me earlier?" I said.

"It was obvious—plus, you fit the part."

"What part?"

"You're an FBI agent, aren't you?"

I laughed.

"Private investigator," I said.

"Private as in hired by someone?"

I nodded.

"And no, it wasn't by your wife," I said.

He turned his head away from me and spit. "I'm tired. Ask your questions. You got five minutes."

"Aren't you interested in who hired me?" I said.

"The only thing I care about right now is getting some sleep. Understand?"

A drop of water splashed on my eyelid and then another one hit my cheek. I looked up at the thick, grey clouds above me.

At some point, Terrence must have noticed the grumbling sky too. He frowned. "Better get on with it."

"Why didn't you like your stepdaughter?" I said.

He shrugged.

"It wasn't her I had a problem with. I don't like kids. Never have. That all?"

"At least you're honest," I said.

"I've got nothing to hide. If I did, I wouldn't be standing here talking to you. Three minutes."

I wondered what he'd do if our conversation went into overtime. Part of me thought it would be fun to find out.

"Why marry Kris if you didn't like kids?" I said.

He turned one of his hands up as if to say I don't know.

"As soon as we met, I knew Kris was the right woman for me. The kid was part of the package. Not much I could do about it. I figured we'd get married, work it all out later."

"Did you ever consider trying to have a relationship with her?"

"The kid?—why? She made it harder for us to, well, do things together. Having her around wasn't very convenient, but what else was I gonna do?"

Jealousy, thy name be Terrence.

"To be honest," he continued, "when the kid went missing, it was kind of a—"

"A what?"

"Doesn't matter. Your time's up."

He hopped in his coupe and shut the door without saying another word. I grabbed the door handle and yanked the door open again.

"What the hell, lady? We're finished."

"I don't understand how Kris could be married to

someone like you. I mean, sure, you seem all professional and in charge at work, but your lack of sympathy for what happened to Olivia amazes me. It almost sounds like you wanted to get rid of her."

Terrence shook his head and smirked. "Those two old crows have been chirping in your ear, haven't they? I was questioned before you came, and I'm sure I'll be questioned again. Difference is—it won't be by you."

CHAPTER FOURTEEN

I wanted to believe there was a special place in hell for men like Terrence. It baffled me how any woman with a child allowed herself to be with a man like him. Kris's self-worth must have plummeted to an all-time low the moment she considered him a decent catch. It saddened and sickened me at the same time, because she knew Terrence never cared about Olivia. Even a woman blinded by love couldn't have missed it. Terrence was a straight-shooter. Kris was desperate. And little Olivia suffered for it. I imagined she spent many nights alone in her room, desperate for attention.

Against my better judgment, I let Maddie choose the restaurant when we reached Jackson Hole, Wyoming. It was late, and I was tired and in desperate need of sleep, but since Maddie was all hopped up on Red Bull, a quiet evening wasn't likely.

After passing two bar and grills and using my behind-the-wheel power of veto, I finally caved when we passed the third dining establishment. My stomach was uneasy, and in need of some form of nourishment. I hoped the place offered some decent sustenance, or we'd be back in the car trying again.

When we walked in and I looked around, I wondered why they hadn't just called the place a bar; I didn't see any evidence of a grill anywhere. There were no double doors suggesting a cooking area in the back, and the closest thing to food on a table was a plastic basket of fries accompanied by a green-colored dipping sauce. It wasn't what I had in mind, but it was too late—Maddie was already on the dance floor whooping it up with a swarm of men who approved of her trashy Wyoming style.

I took a seat at the corner of the bar, trying to fade into the shadows around me. It worked for a few minutes.

A frizzy-haired brunette approached me from behind the bar. "What'll you have to drink?"

"Do you have a menu?"

"I mean to drink, hun?"

"Water."

She snickered, reached under the bar, and slid a laminated, one-sided menu in my direction. I scanned the front side for a viable option, but it didn't matter what I chose. All the items on the menu were dipped in grease and served with a heaping side of grease. Double greasy. I could hardly wait.

Maddie plopped down on the seat next to me, pulled an elastic band off her wrist, and wrapped it around her hair. "C'mon, don't just sit there. Wake up! Let's dance."

"Not tonight," I said. "I'm too tired."

I expected a witty comeback, but she said nothing, and

when I followed her line of sight, I knew why. A tall, well-built man had entered the bar and sat down on the opposite end. He looked like he'd just stepped off Brad Paisley's tour bus in his fringed button-up shirt, tight Wranglers, black boots and matching cowboy hat. But it was his shiny, oversized steer belt buckle that held my attention the most. The horns stuck out so far they could have caused a passerby permanent damage.

Maddie had her eye on a new dance partner.

"Do you mind?" she said.

I smiled.

"Go."

She patted me on the leg. "Be right back."

She hopped off the stool, pulled the rubber band back out, and fluffed her hair with her fingers. She reached Brad Paisley Guy, and a conversation ensued. Strange, but he wasn't looking at her while he was talking—he was staring at me—or at least trying to over the dim-lit lights in the room. Maddie said something, and when he replied, she spun around on her heel and huffed all the way back over to me.

"What did he say?" I said.

"Maybe later."

"Why can't you tell me now?" I said.

"He actually said 'maybe later.'"

"At least it wasn't a no, right?"

But we both knew it was. And Maddie wasn't used to rejection. In an act of defiance, and to increase her no-guy-can-resist-me points, Maddie turned to the man sitting to her left and smiled. He wasted no time buying her a drink.

Brad Paisley Guy approached the DJ, striking up a conversation. They talked for a minute, and then the DJ nodded. The next song started. It was some flip-your-partner-dosey-do kind of thing. I'd never understood the fascination with country dancing and all its flinging and twirling. Maybe it was because I'd never tried it before—I'd never been interested.

"Was you planning on dancing tonight?" a husky voice said.

I turned around, coming face to face with Brad Paisley Guy. "You mean were you?"

He held his hand up to his ear like he couldn't hear me. "Sorry, what? It's a little loud in here."

"You just said 'was' instead of 'were.'" I suddenly felt stupid for pointing it out like I was the bar's grammar police. It didn't matter, I wouldn't ever see him again.

Brad Paisley Guy rolled the toothpick dangling from his lips from one corner of his mouth to the other and squinted. "You're not from around here, are you?"

"Maybe I am—how would you know?"

He took his time looking me up and down like he wanted me to know it. "Nope, you're definitely not a country girl."

His tone didn't seem offensive, but it bothered me anyway.

"Did you want something?" I said

"I'm Cade," he said, tipping his hat forward. "What's your name?"

I pointed to Maddie who was engrossed in her conversation with the man who'd bought her the drink, even though I knew her gift of "ear extend" was on high alert. "That's Maddie."

He laughed. "I meant your name."

"I know what you meant," I said. "Do you have a last name?"

The side of his lip curled up into a smile and he winked. "Sure do. Do you answer everything with a question?"

Before I could say anything else, he placed his hands on my waist, lifted me out of the chair, and dragged me onto the dance floor.

"I don't do this," I said. "Please, don't—"

I tried to back away, but he grabbed my hands, pulling me in until we were so close I could feel his hot, minty breath on my cheek.

"You don't do what, dance?"

"Not country," I said.

He laughed and released one of his hands, wrapping it around my waist. Over the next few minutes I felt like I was sitting in an oversized teacup at a theme park—the kind of ride where at least one person usually threw up before it was over. My body flipped, dipped, and whipped into positions I didn't even know were still possible.

The song ended with me in the dipped position, my head about three inches from the floor. Cade held me there for a few moments, staring into my eyes, but saying nothing.

"Were you going to let me go at some point?" I said.

"Yeah, sorry."

He stood me upright but didn't let go.

"Can I have my hand back too?" I said.

He released me and walked away without saying another word.

What just happened? And why is he walking off? Is it a country/western thing? I didn't know.

"Umm, I think he likes you," Maddie said when I returned to my seat.

"It was one dance," I said, holding up a finger. "Besides, I'm dating Giovanni, and I don't even know the guy."

Maddie nudged me with her shoulder. "He's still looking at you."

I didn't dare look over. "Can we please leave now? I've had enough."

She frowned but took pity on me. A minute later, we were back in the parking lot as if the last hour had never happened.

I said something to Maddie, but she didn't hear me.

"Maddie, are you listening?" I said.

"What? Yeah."

"No, you're not. What are you looking at?"

She pointed to a truck parked under a lamppost. "Nice wheels," Maddie said. "I could see myself with the guy who drives that."

"What are you looking..."

I looked over. It couldn't be—but it was. A truck. A shiny, black Dodge Ram with a grille in the front and Cade gripping the door handle, about to jump inside.

CHAPTER FIFTEEN

Rage consumed me. Cade whatever-his-last-name-was, had been following me. I wanted to yell—scratch that—I wanted to scream, but when my mouth opened, all I could manage was, "You," followed by my pointer finger swirling around in the air like a dagger while I continued to shout, "You—you—you—you—you!"

Cade released the door handle and held his hands up, surrendering to my finger dagger. "Now hold on just a minute, Sloane. Let me explain, okay?"

"No, you hold on! You think you can walk up to me in some bar pretending you've never seen me before in your life, and that's okay?! Why did you ask for my name if you already knew it?"

He smoothed a bit of dirt around with the toe of his boot, like he thought moving a bit of dust would help him decide what to say next. Or not to say.

"You've been following me," I said. "I want to know why."

When he didn't respond, Maddie walked over and stood

next to me, hands on hips. She had no idea what was going on, but it didn't matter. "Sloane asked you a question—I suggest you answer it."

He looked at the two of us like he found the whole thing amusing. "And if I don't?" I placed both hands on the door of his truck, slamming it shut. "You're not going anywhere until I get some answers."

Cade glanced at me and then at Maddie and laughed so hard I thought the toothpick in his mouth would come shooting out. He grabbed it with his hand, flinging it to the ground.

"What's so funny?" I said.

He tossed his hat through the open window of the truck and tipped his head to the side. "You're a lot feistier when you're not on the dance floor. A lot more confident, too."

Maddie and I crossed our arms in synchronized motion and remained silent.

"All right, ladies," he said. "The name's Cade McCoy. Satisfied?"

McCoy? The last name was familiar, but it took me a moment to place it. "As in Walter McCoy, the lead detective in Savannah Tate's case? Are you related?"

He nodded.

"Walter is my dad."

"Is he having you follow me?"

Maddie had a look on her face like she was the only one who hadn't received an invitation to Cade's coming out party. "He's been following you?" She turned to me. "You've been following her? Someone tell me what's going on."

"Not exactly," Cade said.

"Then what exactly?" I said.

"I'm helping my dad."

"Don't you need permission?"

"I got it. The chief and my dad go way back."

"I didn't know stalking me was part of the job description," I said.

"Now hold on. I wasn't trying to scare you."

"You didn't."

Maddie crossed one leg over the other, uncrossed them, and crossed them back again, something she always did when she needed to use the ladies' room.

"Go," I said to her.

"Oh no. I'm not leaving you alone with this—"

"I'll be fine," I said. "But you won't be. Now go."

Once Maddie was out of earshot, Cade said, "I need your help. Tate won't talk to me. My dad says he's been actin' weird lately, like somethin's going on, but he can't get anything out of him."

"What makes you think I can help you?" I said.

"A couple days ago, you met with Tate. He handed you money."

"What you saw was an envelope, nothing more."

He shook his head.

"Do you really think you can bullshit me? You're a private investigator; I know why you're here."

"I don't need a license to snoop around in Wyoming," I said. "Why are you here? This isn't your case; why get involved?"

"My father is retiring in a few months. I'm taking over his position."

It was a bit of a shock, but not unexpected. Although I tried not to show it, I admired Cade for what he was doing. His father needed all the help he could get. "Did you ever consider picking up the phone instead of following me around?"

"I wasn't sure you'd talk to me. Look, solving this case means everything to my father. If there's anything I can do to help him, I will."

I felt like swirling my own foot around in the dirt. The conversation was headed in the direction Cade wanted to take me, but I wasn't sure it would lead to a place I was ready to go.

"You realize I am under no obligation to tell you what I talked about with my client, right?" I said.

"You'll have to if I bring you in."

"Go for it."

"Will you at least tell me why you met with him?"

I shook my head.

"So, you're not willin' to help me at all, then?"

"I work alone," I said.

"And your, uh, friend?"

"Don't let her outgoing nature and lack of a classy dress choice fool you; she's smarter than you think."

"Who's smarter?" came a voice from behind.

"No one, Maddie," I said. "Let's go."

I walked toward the car, stopping a moment to glance back at Cade before getting inside. "Good luck."

"I'd like to know where you're staying—or if you're staying."

"It's none of your concern," I said. "Stop following me."

"You shouldn't even be here."

"I'm not leaving," I said.

"Good. Neither am I."

"Oh, and the next time you want something, don't tail me to try and get it. I don't go for all this sneaking around. People get shot that way."

He nodded.

"Straight shooter, got it."

CHAPTER SIXTEEN

The phone rang. It was Giovanni. I contemplated my options: let it ring, send the call to voicemail, or answer it. It was late, and my eyes were only about twenty-five percent open. I wasn't up for a conversation with anyone, especially him. Still, I wondered where he'd been the past several days. Why he hadn't called, texted, or communicated with me? I wanted answers, but I was too drained to care. I needed sleep. It was his turn to wait.

I tossed the phone to the side and rolled over, appreciating the hotel for using duvets on their beds instead of those cheap tapestry-looking comforters from the eighties. Or was it the seventies? It bugged me that the cover bedding was seldom washed, like slapping on a set of sheets made up for a bedspread that contained more germs per inch than the inside of a frat boy's toilet. I couldn't sleep at night no matter where I was without folding the top sheet over the comforter. It was like a protective layer between me and unwanted germs, and I justified myself by thinking everyone had the same little rituals. Didn't they?

According to a news report I'd seen on TV, the remote and light switches were the areas that contained some of the highest amounts of germs in a hotel room. Since entering, I'd only disinfected the TV remote and the light switch next to my bed. That wasn't too bad, was it? I didn't intend to turn on the bathroom faucets using my elbows or flush the toilet with my foot; I wasn't a germaphobe, I was germ-aware. Big difference.

The phone rang again, which meant Giovanni would keep calling until I answered. He was unstoppable when he wanted something, and I needed sleep. I picked it up.

"Hey," I said.

"Hello, cara mia. It's good to hear your voice."

It was nice to hear his too, but the sweet talk wasn't going to work. Not this time.

"Are you there?" he said.

"I'm here," I said.

"Say something."

"Like what?" I said.

"Anything."

"I don't feel like talking," I said. "I'm tired."

"You're angry. I can hear it in your voice."

"I haven't heard from you in almost a week, Giovanni. Not one word. And now you finally call, and there's no apology, no explanation, nothing. Maybe this is typical relationship behavior for you, but I—"

"I know, I should have told you."

"Told me what?" I said.

"My sister was taken."

"I'm not sure what you mean," I said. "Abducted?"

"Yes."

I couldn't believe it. Another one. Although the reasons wouldn't be the same. Giovanni's sister wasn't a child.

"From where?" I said.

"Her apartment in New York City."

"But she has an alarm system, doesn't she?"

"It was disabled."

"Do you know who did it?"

"My brother and I are working together to figure it out. He's here with me. We're getting close."

Giovanni's brother was in the FBI. If anyone could find her, he could. I wouldn't want to be the other person when they did.

"Why would anyone want to take Daniela?" I said.

There was a pause, followed by heavy breathing.

"Giovanni, I want to know. Tell me."

"I'm afraid it has something to do with me."

"You? Why?"

"A few months ago a group of men I used to do business with reached out to me. They needed a favor, asked for my help. I turned them down. They got angry, started making threats, but I didn't take them seriously. I never believed anything would come of it. I had those closest to me under surveillance, just in case, but—"

"Wait a minute," I said. "You didn't have anyone keeping an eye on me, did you?"

His prolonged silence provided the answer. But I lacked the energy to be angry, and the right—not while Daniela was still missing.

"If you were looking out for your sister, how did she get abducted?" I said.

"That's what I've been trying to figure out. It appears one of my men may have been providing information to someone else."

"Who?"

"I have my suspicions, and he is being followed. I need to be sure."

"Why did you wait so long to tell me?" I said.

"I didn't want to get you involved—this is something I need to do on my own."

"You involved me when I became part of your life," I said.

"I knew you'd be right beside me, which is why I waited to tell you until you had a new case. I've put Daniela in danger; I won't let it happen to you as well."

"How do you know about my case?"

Stupid question. He knew everything, except for the current whereabouts of his sister. And he was right. If I hadn't been trying to find Olivia and Savannah, I would have been on the next flight to New York City.

Giovanni apologized, something he wasn't used to doing. It was sincere, and as much as I wanted to be there, he promised to keep me informed of any progress he was making if I stayed put, and I agreed—at least until my own case was solved. But if I solved it, and Daniela was still missing, our deal was off.

"It was me," Maddie said when my conversation with

Giovanni was over. She sat down on the bed, patting Lord Berkeley on the head and avoiding eye contact. "Lucio called me and wanted to know if you were all right."

I leaned back on the pillow. "Well, at least now I know why Giovanni finally called. Once he found out I had something else to occupy my time, he knew I wouldn't fly out there. Not right now, anyway."

"He just didn't want you to worry," she said.

But I was worried, and not just for Daniela. I was finally starting to understand the consequences of being involved with someone who lived the kind of life Giovanni did. He might have been loving and kind to me, but that was only one side of his personality. I'd never seen the other. And I didn't want to—I'd grown fond of him over the past several months, an attribute that allowed me to overlook certain things. I couldn't imagine what Daniela might have been suffering on her brother's behalf, or if she was still alive. I wanted to sleep, but I couldn't. Now that I knew the price of being with him, what was I going to do about it?

CHAPTER SEVENTEEN

In my dream, two girls were running through the woods, calling for me—by name. The sounds of their voices echoed around me. The girls came to a door suspended in mid-air between two giant pine trees and knocked on it, even though they could have just stepped around it and been on the other side. I tried to open the door, but it was stuck. The knob turned, but when I pulled back, nothing happened. Their knocking grew so loud it vibrated in my head, forcing me awake.

Someone was knocking on the hotel room door.

I sat straight up in bed and looked around. I shouted for Maddie. There was no reply. And Boo wasn't on the bed anymore. Maybe Maddie had gone out and forgotten her room key. I threw my robe on and cracked open the door, surprised when it wasn't Maddie on the other side.

The man in the hallway was an older gentleman, at least twenty years my senior, maybe more. He wore a button-up shirt with a thin, black vest over the top, and a brown cowboy hat that looked like it had gone through the washing machine

a few too many times. Around his neck was a tassel-like
choker worn in place of a tie with a round piece of solid rock
the size of a half dollar dangling from it. His beard was white
and slight and most likely trimmed on a daily basis. It made
him look respectable and refined, but it didn't hide his tired,
stress-infused eyes.

"Detective McCoy?" I said.

"How'd you know?" the man said with a slight smile.

"Lucky guess," I said. "You're Cade's father, right?"

He nodded. "I was hopin' I could have a word?"

I stifled a yawn. "What time is it?"

"A little after six in the mornin'," he said. "I'm sorry if I
woke you. I can come back later if you like."

I opened the door all the way, letting him in. "Give me
just a minute."

I brushed my teeth, saving my daily flossing routine for
later. I didn't want to keep the detective waiting. On the
bathroom counter was a note scratched in pencil:

I took Boo for a walk. Back soon.

I pulled on a pair of jeans, zipped up my sweater, and
joined the detective in the living room area of the hotel.

"My son says you're a private investigator," he said.

"Are you here to ask me to leave? Because if you are, you
should know I—"

He shook his head.

"Six months ago, I would have done everything in my
power to run you out of town, but now..." He curled one
hand over the other, resting them in his lap. "My boy says you

had a meetin' with Noah Tate a few days ago. I'm interested in knowin' what the conversation was all about."

I crossed one leg over the other. "I'm sure you're aware of why Mr. Tate came to see me."

Detective McCoy removed his hat and placed it on the cushion beside him. "I am."

"Then what you're really asking me is whether I know something you don't."

He sighed.

"S'pose so." He leaned back, tugging on a bit of chin hair. "Well, do you?"

"There is one thing," I said.

Detective McCoy's eyes electrified, almost changing color. "What did he tell you?"

"I can't say right now," I said. "Not yet."

Detective McCoy contemplated my statement like he was trying to decide what he should do next, which was fine with me. I wasn't going to tell him either way.

"In all my years of police work, I've never had a case like this," he said. "Sure, there have been a few murders now and again, but not more than I can count on one hand, and none I couldn't solve. The responsible party has always been obvious. I thought that's how I'd retire. I'd go out like all the others before me, quiet and unnoticed, without ever having the kind of case that keeps a man up all night wonderin' if he'd missed something."

He hung his head and continued.

"Do you want to know somethin'? For a while, I actually felt a little like I'd been robbed, not havin' a case like this, until

I got it. Now I'd do anything to go out as the quiet guy. I feel incapable of doing the job I was sworn in to do. I can't go anywhere in this town without feelin' like I've let everyone down. I can see it in their eyes every time they look at me. I've gotten to know Savannah Tate so well over the months, I feel like she's my own child."

The emotions of others had always been hard for me to endure. As a child, the verbal tongue-lashing my sister and I received from our father, combined with the physical abuse he unleashed on my mother, shut me down almost completely, and I never felt like I'd fully restarted. I wasn't devoid of feelings—I'd always felt an iota of something—but it seemed like it wasn't ever the same thing other people felt.

"Detective McCoy, I don't mind sharing what I know. In fact, I want you to know. I just need to speak with Mr. Tate first."

"When do you plan on seeing him next?" he said.

"I'll be stopping by his house today. Can we meet up again this evening?"

He grabbed his hat and stood up, pleased with the progress he'd made. He took out his wallet and handed me his card. "My home number is there," he said, pointing. "It's the best way to reach me. I'm not much for cell phones. I have one, but I forget to charge the damn thing."

I nodded and accepted the card.

Detective McCoy hesitated a moment.

"Is there anything else?" I said.

"You'll have to forgive my boy," he said. "Cade's having a hard time seeing me go through all of this. But he doesn't mean you any harm. He's just trying to help his old man."

"Cade said he'll be taking over your position."

"Looks like it," he said.

"Have you worked together long?"

He shook his head.

"Cade went into law enforcement right out of high school, but then he got married and decided to move away."

"Why?"

"His wife," he said. "She was determined to live by her family. She didn't want much to do with ours. I never understood why. But back then, Cade didn't deny her anything. He would have moved anywhere just to make her happy."

How very codependent of him.

"And now? How does she feel about living here?"

"Cade's wife walked out on him a couple years back. Took off with some guy she'd met at work. Left Cade to raise their daughter on his own. That woman just walked out. No note, no warning. She didn't even bother taking her things. Not that I'm complaining. Finally gives his mother and me the chance to get to know our granddaughter. I'm not gonna lie, we're glad he's home."

The world had changed in a profound way since my grandparents were young. Back then people fought for their marriage, worked things out, didn't give up on each other so easily. People respected each other. They worked hard, and it wasn't easy, but they were happy. Most of the time, anyway. That's what my grandpa had always said.

But things had changed. The world had changed. Men

and women were impatient and selfish and rushed. They didn't like it when things didn't "feel" right. But instead of taking a long, hard look at themselves and accepting responsibility for their part in the relationship, they fled the scene. At the first sign of trouble, they simply ended things, walked out. Men succumbed to the temptation of another woman, and women abandoned their own children, leaving them for someone else to raise. It was all about me, me, me. There was some level of independence that came with this, but no balance.

Of course everyone didn't give up so easily, but it was happening all around me: to my friends, my neighbors, my loved ones. I didn't understand how anyone could behave in such a disrespectful, selfish way and still feel good about themselves. Maybe because it wasn't in me to do those things. I wasn't a quitter. My relationships hadn't always worked out, but when they ended, they ended honorably, and not because I'd been brainwashed into thinking life could be better in someone else's bed.

CHAPTER EIGHTEEN

Mr. Tate had the kind of home that made me question what he did for a living and whether Harrison Ford's eight-hundred-acre ranch was anywhere nearby, but there were no signs, no Hollywood tour buses, nothing to indicate the Indiana Jones star even lived around there. Maybe that's what attracted Mr. Tate to the area in the first place. It was quiet and had neighborhoods that reminded me a lot of Park City—with the exception of the magnificent Grand Tetons in the background.

The exterior of his home was made of part stone and part wood, although I couldn't tell what kind of wood. It was unlike anything I'd ever seen before. A detached garage sat to the left of the house, and judging from its size, a half a dozen cars could have fit in it. On the front of the house an American flag was bolted into one of the two square wood columns on the porch.

Everything about the area was perfect, except for the black Dodge Ram parked across the street. Obviously my message from the previous evening had not been received. The two of us exited our vehicles at the same time. But Cade was the only person with a smile on his face.

"Mornin'," he said. "You look…rested."

"What are you doing here?"

"I knew you'd show up sooner or later," he said.

"What if it was later?"

He shrugged.

"I would have waited. It's not like I have other pressin' matters to attend to right now."

"If Noah Tate was interested in talking to you, he wouldn't have hired me. What do you plan to achieve by hanging around?"

"I figure if anyone can get him to talk to me, it's you," he said, pointing in my direction.

"I wouldn't stick around to find out if I were you."

He folded his arms.

"You want to find Savannah, don't you? So do I—so does my dad." He threw his arms in the air. "Hell, so does everyone. I've been thinkin', maybe if you can get him to talk, I'll let you work with me."

He'd let me? I tried to stifle the laugh I felt coming on.

"No thanks. I'll pass."

"Now don't be hasty," he said. "Just give it some time, let it simmer awhile before you make your final decision. We can talk more about it later."

"I don't need your help. And I'm not going anywhere until you leave."

Cade shoved his hands in his pockets and leaned back against the truck, allowing his cowboy hat to fall past his eyes. "Suit yourself."

I felt the urge to throw a temper tantrum.

"What are you doing?"

"Sleepin', I'm tired." He winked at me. "You let me know when you change your mind, now."

"I won't, so you'd better—"

"Sloane?"

I turned.

Noah Tate approached us from behind. "What are you doing here—and who's this?" he said, thumbing at Cade.

Before I could respond Cade's hand shot forward. "Pleased to finally meet you, Mr. Tate. I'm Cade McCoy."

Mr. Tate didn't shake hands. He didn't move. Without looking at me he said, "Next time you want to ambush me like this, Miss Monroe, call first!"

A few seconds later his front door slammed shut with a bang, locking us outside.

"Nice job," I said. "Now he won't talk to me either."

Cade pulled on the tailgate of his truck. He eased it down and sat on the edge, patting the area next to him, like I'd be happy to oblige. I didn't.

"Maybe we don't need him to talk to us," he said.

"Trust me, we do."

He grinned.

"Is this the part where you tell me what you wouldn't tell my dad?"

I crossed my arms.

"It isn't."

Several minutes went by. I stood, Cade sat. I passed the time by trying to decide how I could get Mr. Tate to let me into his house so I could somehow convince him to turn over the letter without involving any more people than I had to.

"It's been ten minutes," Cade said. "You got a plan?"

I shook my head.

"Yeah, you do," he said. "I can tell."

"You stay here. Let me try and talk to him."

Cade scooted off the tailgate.

I warned. "Take one more step and I'm leaving, and you can handle Mr. Tate on your own. You've been doing a great job so far."

"Relax," Cade said, spreading his hands out to the side. "Geez. I'm going to get in my truck. I'll even close the door if it makes you feel better. Maybe that'll help things. You can even tell him I'm leavin' if you like."

We both knew it wasn't true.

I approached the front door and knocked. Nothing happened. I tried again. Still nothing, and there was no sound coming from inside, even though I knew at least one person was there. On the third try, the door cracked open. A small child around three years old peeked out.

"Hi," she said softly.

"How are you?" I said.

"My daddy's mad."

"What's your name?" I said.

She looked down at her hands and whispered, "Lily."

I knelt down until we were eye level. I'd heard once that little kids were more receptive and comfortable when adults didn't tower over them like giants. Kids felt better when an adult lowered themselves to their level. "It's nice to meet you,

Lily. My name is Sloane. I'm a friend of your dad's. Do you think you could get him for me?"

She glanced to the side, opening the door. "Come on."

"Oh, sweetie, I don't know if I should—"

"Come on, come on!" she insisted.

Lily turned and skipped down the hall yelling, "Daddy… daddy…daddy."

But daddy didn't come. So I went to him. I found Mr. Tate in his office, his eyes glued to a magazine, even though he wasn't reading, not really. I made a fist and tapped gently on the open door.

"You're fired, Miss Monroe. You have no right being in my house. Please go."

I sat in a chair across from him. "Hand over the coloring page and I will."

"It's no longer in my possession."

"Of course it is," I said. "You wouldn't let a precious item like that out of your sight. Give it to me and spare your family the embarrassment of having your house searched. Once the police know what you have and how it links up with the other kidnapping, they'll get a warrant, and you'll have cops all over this place. Is that what you want?"

He sighed.

"It doesn't concern you anymore."

"Of course it does," I said. "I keep my word, Mr. Tate. And we had a deal. Firing me doesn't change anything."

He hurled the magazine to the side of his desk, but his aim was weak. It slid off the side, falling to the floor. I picked it up and set it down in front of him.

"I thought I was hiring a private investigator," he said. "Obviously, I was mistaken. You said you wouldn't involve the police."

"I haven't."

Not yet.

He pointed toward the window. "That McCoy kid is the police, is he not?"

I nodded.

"He's the one who's been trying to talk to you. And just so we're clear, I was as surprised as you when he showed up here today. If you spent two seconds listening to our conversation, you would have understood I was only trying to convince him to leave."

Mr. Tate raised a brow. "What's he doing here?" he said.

"Cade followed you the other day. He saw us meet at the restaurant and watched you hand me the money."

"He followed me?"

"He's trying to take over things for his dad."

Mr. Tate's shoulders relaxed and he leaned forward in his chair. In a lowered voice he said, "Why?"

"Detective McCoy Senior is retiring. Cade will be assuming his position, and he had some crazy idea that if he showed up here with me, you'd give him a chance. After today, they'll be involved whether you like it or not, but how you choose to go about it is up to you."

I heard a swishing sound like sandpaper being scraped across a wood floor. Mr. Tate shifted his gaze from me to a woman standing in the doorway. She was pale and thin, and her hair was matted, as if it hadn't been brushed in days.

"Noah, what's going on?" She gazed in my direction. "Who's she?"

Mr. Tate rose from his chair, a look of genuine concern and guilt on his face. "No one, honey. Go back to bed, okay?"

"Mommy, I'm hungry," Lily said, pulling on the ruffle of the woman's nightgown.

"Mommy's tired now, Lily," Mr. Tate said. "Go play, and I'll make you a sandwich in a few minutes."

"But I don't want a sandwich," Lily said, stomping her foot on the ground, "mac and cheese, mac and cheese!"

"I don't have time for that, sweetheart," Mr. Tate said.

"I do," I said.

All three of them looked over at me, understandably stunned.

At that moment, the doorbell rang. I had no doubt about who was on the other side of the door.

Sit in his vehicle and wait, my ass.

Mrs. Tate gripped the side of the door so tight I thought if she let go, her knees would buckle and she'd tumble to the ground.

"Miss Monroe, I'm sorry to ask," Mr. Tate said, "especially after the way I've treated you today, but do you think you could help my wife back to her room?" He pointed toward the hallway. "It's the last door on the left."

I nodded, looked at Lily, and said, "I'm going to take your mommy back to her room, and when I'm done, we'll see about making some macaroni and cheese, okay?"

The idea of a stranger offering to cook a meal was apparently too much for Lily to comprehend. She covered her eyes with her hands, pretending I wasn't there, and then backed out of the room, her Dora the Explorer slippers bouncing up and down as she turned and ran down the hall. I didn't blame her one bit.

I swung my arm around Mrs. Tate who clung to the door jamb at first, not willing to let go. Once she realized I wasn't going away, she released her grip and sagged into me. We advanced down the hallway until we both stood next to her bed. I pulled the covers down so she could settle in, but she didn't. She just stood there, staring at me. I didn't say anything. She didn't say anything.

I could tell she'd internalized so much over the past six months, she didn't know how to let her emotions out. I opened my mouth to offer some kind of sentiment and she slapped me—hard—across my left cheek. Then she slapped me again across my right. I should have been stunned, but I wasn't. I got it. I wrapped my hands around her wrists, holding them out in front of her, making sure not to grip them too tightly. She didn't know who I was, and she didn't care. I was there because of Savannah, and I wasn't doing anything. No one was, not in her eyes. She was in pain, and she wanted everyone else to feel it too.

I looked at her and said the only thing I could say. "I'm sorry."

A wave of shame and regret spread across her face once she realized what she'd done. My face was hot. It felt like I'd burned my cheeks after sitting in the sun for too long. For a woman as frail as she was, she knew how to deliver a slap with an intense sting.

Mrs. Tate sniffled and then the tears came. First it was just a few, but by the time I released her wrists, she was crying uncontrollably. I just stood there, watching her stick her right hand in her pocket and pull it out, over and over again, like she had no control over her own limb. Every time it went in, she touched something before pulling it out again, but I couldn't see what it was.

I helped Mrs. Tate into bed and then found some tissue so she could wipe her eyes. I held it out to her. She clutched something in her right hand. It looked like a piece of paper no bigger than the size of a mini notebook. She pressed it against her chest and began rocking back and forth, mumbling something I couldn't understand. I tried to get her to lie down, but she shook her head furiously. I backed off.

When the rocking slowed, her eyelids began to open and shut, each time getting heavier until they no longer opened. I pulled the blankets up to her neck, making sure to fold the sheet over the top. Then I reached for the paper that had slipped out of her hand. It was a photograph of her and her missing daughter. It was bent and worn, like she'd been holding it for days, months even. In the photo, she looked like a completely different person. Her hair was long and lustrous, and she had a radiant smile. The photo depicted a woman with a fulfilling, invigorating life. She looked nothing like the person she was today.

The top drawer of the nightstand was cracked open just enough for me to glimpse inside. I did and then shifted my focus to the wide array of pill bottles lining the top of the nightstand. They were in all shapes and sizes. Some were in bottles, others in cardboard boxes, and a few were scattered around like they'd been spilled and no one had bothered to clean them up. The entire scene was grave. Mrs. Tate was barely clinging to life. The hope that her daughter was still out there somewhere was the only thing keeping her alive.

CHAPTER NINETEEN

After making macaroni and cheese for maybe the third or fourth time in my life, I joined Mr. Tate and Cade in the living room. They were engaged in a civil conversation, which gave me a small assurance that the two of them might be able to work together after all.

Cade glanced at me when I walked in. "Mr. Tate has agreed to answer my questions, but only if you're present."

"I thought I was fired," I said.

"You know I didn't mean it," Mr. Tate replied.

I sat next to Cade, but not too close.

"Ask your questions."

The next several minutes passed by in a mundane manner, with Cade asking many of the same questions Mr. Tate had grown not-so-fond-of. At one point, he looked like he was ready to shut down and show Cade the door, but he maintained his composure, keeping a straight face. He wasn't smiling, but he wasn't frowning, either. It wasn't until Cade asked him if there was anything else he should know that Mr. Tate shifted his position in his seat and looked over at me.

"What have you found out since our meeting?" Mr. Tate said to me.

"Someone saw Olivia Hathaway in the parking lot the day she was taken."

Cade's forehead wrinkled in confusion. It was fine with me. Let him wonder. He deserved it.

"Why didn't the person come forward when it happened?" Tate said.

I said, "It was a young boy. He was embarrassed because he didn't do anything to keep it from happening. But I've convinced him to give a statement to the police."

Once Todd realized I wasn't going to leave him alone, he talked to his parents, and the three of them went to the police. At the pleading of his mother, the detectives promised to keep Todd's name out of the papers—maybe not forever, but for now.

"How good was the description the boy gave?" Mr. Tate said.

"He remembered enough to get a sketch artist on it. He also knows the make and model of the vehicle the man was driving."

"Unbelievable," Mr. Tate said.

I looked at a still-confused Cade and then back at Tate. "You know what you have to do now."

Cade turned one of his palms up and shook his head. "What is going on between you two?"

"I've got something I need to show you," Mr. Tate said. "But I'd like your father to be here when I do."

Detective McCoy arrived a half hour later looking far more haggard than he had earlier that morning. He apologized, saying he thought he was coming down with something. By the looks of him, he'd already come down with it.

Mr. Tate paced the floor like he was preparing to give the most important speech of his life. It wasn't until he realized all eyes were on him and no one else was talking that he started in with his story. Cade and his father listened while Mr. Tate talked about his theory on the correlation between the two kidnappings. Then he switched gears, mentioning the coloring page he'd received in the mail. Detective McCoy seemed relieved the truth was finally coming out, but Cade looked like he wanted to blacken both of Tate's eyes for withholding evidence. When Mr. Tate finished, no one said anything for a long time.

"At least we are all on the same page now," I said. "Once the two cases come together, maybe we can find these girls."

I hoped, alive. It was a lot to wish for, but I didn't want to accept the worst until I had no other choice.

Cade shook his head. "What a mess."

"We'll have to get with the boys in Sublette County and sort all this stuff out," Detective McCoy said. "Since we may have mutual interests, my hope is we can swap information with each other."

He rose from the sofa and winced, placing a hand on his lower back and holding it there. When he caught me staring, his hand dropped to his side. "If you all will excuse me, I better call the chief and tell him what's going on."

Once Detective McCoy was out of the room, Cade started in on Mr. Tate. "How could you keep this critical piece of evidence from my father?"

Mr. Tate looked at me, but I didn't want to interfere. Not yet. My turn was coming.

"Olivia's parents said they never got the picture back once they handed it over to the police," Mr. Tate said. "And once they had it, they still couldn't find her, so why should I trust it with you?"

"It could help us find your daughter and the other girl, Olivia," Cade said. "What good does it do sitting here in your house?"

"It helps my wife—gives her peace, gives her hope."

Cade threw his hands in the air. "Hope for what? Your wife barely gets out of bed anymore!"

The words slipped out of Cade's mouth just as Lily's sweet face poked around the corner. I placed a hand on Cade's arm and squeezed just enough for him to stop before it got any worse.

"I'll be outside," he whispered to me. "I can't believe you knew about this and didn't say anything. What was you thinkin'?"

"We'll discuss this later," I said. "Away from here."

"Get the flippin' paper, or whatever it is."

I nodded.

Mr. Tate had already left the room, apparently to get the paper. When he returned, he said, "I hope you don't get in trouble because of me."

"I'm sure I can handle it."

He handed the folded page to me. "There was an envelope, but I can't find it. I swear. I saw it yesterday, but now it's gone. Maybe my wife knows, but she's sleeping right now, and I don't want to—"

I took the paper from him and smiled. "No worries," I said. "When you find it, let me know. In the meantime, I'll make sure they get this."

Mr. Tate closed his eyes. He looked worried. I didn't know if it was because the envelope was missing, or if it had to do with something else. If it was over the envelope, he was fretting over nothing. I knew exactly where it was.

CHAPTER TWENTY

"Where's the rest of it?" Cade said.

I shrugged, handing him the coloring page.

"This is all he gave to me."

Cade dangled the plastic baggie in front of me. "Paper doesn't come in the mail without an envelope."

"He said he'll try to find it."

Cade slid into the seat of his truck, started the engine, and snatched his cowboy hat from the seat next to him. He put it on and said, "It doesn't matter. Once they get a warrant, they'll find it, along with whatever else the man has been hiding."

"Why don't you bring that high horse of yours down a couple notches?" I said. "They're suffering. Do you really want to rip their entire home apart for an envelope? Your father certainly has told you what Mrs. Tate is going through—she's barely coherent."

Cade whipped his head around, staring at me. "Are you done giving me advice? If I want to know how you feel, I'll ask."

I felt an uncomfortable pain in my stomach over a man I'd just met.

He pulled the truck door shut and sped out of the driveway, leaving me alone with his father who had taken it all in like we were shooting the main scene of an old movie.

"I guess I'll be seeing you later, maybe," Detective McCoy said.

The way the words came out of his mouth was awkward—like he didn't really know what to say, but he felt compelled to say something.

"Have you told him yet?" I said.

"I don't follow."

"That you're sick," I said.

"Why would I—it's just a nasty virus. It'll pass."

"But it won't, will it?" I said.

My accusation caught him off guard.

"What makes you say that?"

"You grabbed your back when you stood up in Mr. Tate's house. And when you came by my hotel room this morning, I noticed your eyes. Even though it was early, they looked a bit yellow to me."

Part of me was sorry for prying—whatever he was going through wasn't my business.

Detective McCoy walked over to where I was standing and looked at me. "You assume a lot, Miss Monroe."

"Am I wrong?"

There was a long pause and then he said, "Do you think Cade knows?"

"I'm not sure. I don't know your son very well. How's he

been acting since he moved back here?"

"Fine. A little on edge, maybe. But I just thought it had to do with the case, or looking after his teenage daughter. He's got a lot of his own things he's dealing with right now. I didn't want to add one more thing to the list."

"Do you mind me asking what's wrong?" I said.

"Pancreatic cancer."

"Are you getting treatment for it?"

He shook his head.

"Too late for that now. I felt fine at first, and by the time I realized something was wrong, the doctor told me it had spread. It's too late to operate—too late to do anything but sit and wait to die. Doesn't seem fair, but I suppose nothin' ever does."

I wanted to say something, but what could I say to a person who knew he was going to die? I was a fixer. I liked to fix things, make things whole again. I didn't know how to be any other way.

"You won't tell my boy, will you?" he said.

I grabbed Mr. McCoy's hand, a gesture that shocked both of us. "Of course not. It's not my secret to tell."

He smiled.

"You know what? I like you, Miss Monroe. I like you a lot."

I liked him too.

CHAPTER TWENTY-ONE

"Is it possible to lift a print from an envelope?" I said.

Maddie held her hand out. "Anything's possible, sweetie. What do you have for me?"

I took the envelope out of my bag, using a tissue to handle the edges and handed it to her. "Sorry, I didn't have time to put it in anything. I just grabbed it."

She read the address on the front and peeked inside. "Where's the rest of it?"

"Cade McCoy has it. They're probably processing it now."

"And you didn't want this processed along with it?"

I ran a hand through my hair. "I don't know. I wasn't really thinking. I saw it inside the top drawer of Mrs. Tate's nightstand, and I couldn't resist. I knew I had to leave the coloring page, but I thought I could get away with nabbing this part, so I did."

She raised a brow. "All righty, then."

"Can you do anything with it without being at your lab? I doubt we have access to the chemicals you'd need here."

She raised a finger. "There is another way—a new

technique we've been using lately in the lab. Believe it or not, I can get prints off this by using a ceramic hair straightener."

"You're not serious?" I said.

"Completely.   I'll need my glasses to see the prints though."

"You don't wear glasses," I said.

"I'm not talking about regular glasses. They're special goggles with orange lenses. Under a certain light, I'll be able to see the prints. It would probably be easier just to mail this to my guys and let them do it, but then we run the risk of this getting lost somewhere along the way, not to mention what could happen if one of my guys screws up."

"They know what they're doing, don't they?" I said.

"Lifting prints from paper is delicate. If the straightener is on the paper for too long, the paper turns brown, and the prints are lost. Once that happens, there are no do-overs. They're lost forever."

I sighed.

"I shouldn't have taken it," I said. "Even if you get a print that doesn't belong to you, me, the mailman, the processors at the post office, and Mr. and Mrs. Tate, you still can't run it. Not here."

It was like my brain was running on half a cylinder. I was practical, not irrational. I thought things through. I didn't talk first and think later. My words were orchestrated, almost rehearsed. So what the hell was I doing?

"Well, it's too late now," Maddie said. "What do you want me to do with this?"

I shook my head.

"I don't know."

Maddie grabbed a container out of her suitcase, emptied it out, and placed the envelope inside. Then she shoved it into her purse. "While you're thinking about things, I'll go pick us up some dinner."

Maddie scooped Lord Berkeley up with one hand and walked out the door. I stripped down to nothing and stepped into the shower. I stood beneath the faucet wishing the moisture could wash away a lot more than a few flecks of dirt. In some ways, I felt I was getting somewhere locating the missing girls. I'd found a new witness and convinced Mr. Tate to turn over the drawing. But in other ways, I wasn't anywhere near finding the answers. Maybe that's why I'd taken the envelope in the first place. I wanted to grasp at something, even if it was the wrong thing.

I thought about Giovanni and wondered if he'd found his sister yet. I should have been there helping him, even if he didn't want me to—but I was committed to finding Olivia and Savannah. I couldn't stop now.

I turned the water off and reached around the shower curtain for my towel. I dried off, wrapped the towel around me, and stepped out. A hand grabbed at my arm, slapping a handcuff around my wrist. I looked up. Cade McCoy lifted my cuffed hand into the air and snapped the other half of the cuff around the shower rod. Not the greatest idea, but since it was bolted into the wall on both sides and the rod appeared to be industrial-strength, it wouldn't be the easiest thing to get out of. And he knew what he was doing. He'd wrapped it so tight, even with my small wrists there was no way for me to break free.

"What are you doing?!" I said.

"Where's the envelope, Sloane?"

"What?"

"I know you took it from Tate's house." He dangled a key in front of my face. "Tell me where it is, and I'll unlock you."

"I don't have it," I said.

He shrugged.

"Guess I have no choice—I'll have to find it myself."

He walked out of the bathroom. A moment later I heard the sound of various items being strewn around the bedroom.

"How dare you—you can't just go through my things!" I said. "What right do you—"

He stuck his head into the bathroom and winked. "You wanna stop me, go right ahead."

The nerve of him breaking into my hotel room and rifling through my personal items was too much for me. I braced myself against the wall and tugged on the cuffs, using every muscle at my disposal. They wouldn't budge.

Cade burst out laughing.

"It's not funny!" I shouted.

"Not to you maybe, but it is to me. How long do you think it'll take you to get out of those?"

"Maddie will be back any minute, and then we'll see if you still find it so amusing."

"No, she won't."

"What do you mean?" I said.

"I saw her down at the Chinese place a few minutes ago. Paid my friend a few bucks to uh, keep her busy for a while.

She's easily distracted, so I'd say I have all the time I need."

"You could have just talked to me. You didn't have to hold me against my will."

"I've tried talking to you," he said. "It never works. Thanks for the suggestion, though. I'll keep it in mind for next time."

Drawers opened and closed, and then Cade walked somewhere else. I heard the sound of papers shuffling around, followed by the unzipping of a suitcase. So much for privacy.

"Stay out of my bag—you can't go through my personal items!"

"You know, Sloane, this would be a lot easier if you'd just told me where I could find it," he said.

"Fine. Let me out of these cuffs, and I will."

"Oh, no. Somethin' tells me once you're released, you might have a change of heart."

He was getting ready to experience that change of heart first-hand. While he'd been sifting and sorting, I'd used my foot to inch over a sewing kit on the bathroom counter, a complimentary item provided by the hotel. Once it was close enough, I slid the plastic lid open with my hand, carefully and quietly pulling out the needle inside.

"You give up yet?" Cade shouted.

I thought about turning on the waterworks, but even I wouldn't buy that. "I have nothing to say to you. I'd appreciate it if you'd stop talking."

"Works for me," he said.

I lifted the needle into the air, lining it up with the hole on the cuff around my wrist. All I had to do now was stick it in, make sure it was in the correct position, and I was free.

"What do you think you're doin'?" Cade said.

The needle dropped as I glanced up. Defeated. Cade was inches from my face, staring down at me. My damp, soggy hair splashed droplets of water into my eyes, probably causing my mascara to run. I knew I should have scrubbed it off in the shower. I imagined I resembled one of the female zombies in Shaun of the Dead. No wonder he'd been laughing. Cade smelled like a mixture of spices and some kind of wood, which I shouldn't have found intoxicating, but I couldn't help it.

He leaned in, and I leaned back.

What was he doing?

"You know, you're very pretty," he said. "Even with all the wet hair in your face."

"Don't talk to me," I said. But it was more of a whisper than a demand.

He raised his arms, and a moment later, my hand was free. I considered slapping him across the face but tended to my throbbing wrist instead. There was plenty of time to slap him later. Cade stepped back, fully prepared for me to strike. He was perplexed when I didn't.

"Wait—that's it?" he said. "I was prepared for some kind of retaliation. What's gotten into you?"

The door to the hotel room had opened, and it took no time for Lord Berkeley to realize something was amiss. He bounded into the bathroom, teeth clenched, barking loud enough for five floors of guests to hear.

I looked at Cade.

"I suggest you don't touch him. He may be small, but don't let his size fool you."

Cade nodded.

Maddie walked into the bathroom and came to a standstill, taking in the scene around her. The handcuffs were still dangling from the shower rod, and with me in nothing but a towel and Cade staring at me, key in hand, I could only imagine what she was thinking.

"I, umm, don't really know what's going on here, but ahh, do you two want me to go?" she said, pointing at the door.

I shook my head and reached down, scooping up Lord Berkeley. "Maddie stay, Cade go."

"Can I say one thing before I leave?" Cade said.

"You've said enough, and you've done enough," I said. "I'd like to get dressed now."

He walked out, closing the door behind him.

I was relieved Cade hadn't thought to ask Maddie about the envelope. He simply left the room like I'd asked.

A giggling Maddie looked at me and said, "You wanna tell me what that was all about?"

So I did.

CHAPTER TWENTY-TWO

When I was sixteen, I was hired by a family on my street to watch their seven-year-old daughter, Anna. Both parents worked. And before I came along, I heard they'd left her alone from time to time while they ran what they liked to call "short" errands. But some of those errands lasted for hours. At least, that's what the neighbors told my mother during one of their gossip sessions.

I was thrilled to earn some extra money, but developing a relationship with Anna was like trying to befriend a dog who wasn't loyal to anyone but his owners. I couldn't get her to talk to me. She wasn't shy; it was like she didn't trust anyone. I tried different things with her, even taking her to the movies once. In the middle of the show, she said she wanted more popcorn. She knew where the concession counter was, and hadn't wanted me to come with her. So I sat there. Five minutes passed and then ten. I went to check on her and couldn't find her anywhere. She wasn't in the building. One of the workers said he'd filled up her popcorn and then she walked out of the movie theater. The feeling of fear that I had about losing her was more intense than anything I'd ever experienced in my entire life.

Anna had decided to walk home. I found her on a sidewalk a couple blocks away, cold and shaking. It took some convincing, but I finally managed to get her inside the car.

When we arrived back at Anna's house, her father questioned her about why she left the theater without telling me. She wouldn't answer, so he pulled her pants down in front of me, spanking her with his bare hand. I thought it would just be once, but then he did it again, this time becoming more enraged.

When Anna's father raised his hand a third time, she looked at me, and in a trembling voice, she said my name. Up until then, I wasn't even sure she knew what it was. She'd never said it before. I'll never forget how she looked at me, like I was the only one in her life who understood what her life was like. And I did. Her father was a lot bigger than me, of course. But sometimes people underestimate how strong another person can be, especially once the adrenalin starts flowing. No one could stop me, not even him. I yanked her off his knee, tore out of the house with her in tow, and ran all the way to my house, both of us too terrified to look back until we got there.

I never babysat for Anna's parents again, but I did tell my mother what had happened, and since she had been a victim of abuse herself during her marriage to my father, she had zero tolerance when it came to letting it happen to anyone else, especially when that person was a child. She tried to talk to Anna's mother, and when that didn't work, she made some phone calls. I didn't see Anna again after that day. I asked my mom what had happened, and the only thing she said was she'd taken care of it. Anna was safe.

Some people shouldn't have kids.

I thought about that as I watched the minutes tick by on the digital clock on the nightstand. I'd tried to sleep for hours, but I couldn't quiet my mind. It was filled with the mental images I'd created of Olivia and Savannah and the sorrow I felt for what their families were going through.

The soft melody coming from my iPhone pulled me out of my thoughts. The time was now three-something in the morning. Only one of my eyes was functioning properly, so I couldn't be sure of the time.

Maddie grunted in disgust. "Who calls at this hour?"

I didn't move. Was the phone actually ringing?

Maddie chucked a pillow in my direction. "Are you going to answer it, or what?"

"Hello?" I said.

"Miss Monroe?"

"Who's this?" I said.

"Noah Tate."

But it didn't sound like Mr. Tate at all.

"It's early, Mr. Tate," I said. "Is everything okay?"

"No—it's not. It's my wife, Jane."

As soon as he'd said his wife's name, I knew everything wasn't okay. I knew everything wasn't going to be okay ever again. By the time Maddie and I parked at the hospital and went in, it was already too late. Jane Tate was dead. She'd woken up at some point in the night, taken about ten too many pills, and went back to sleep, this time for all eternity. Even if I did find Savannah, and even if she was still alive, their family wouldn't ever be together. Not in this lifetime.

Mr. Tate came stumbling into the waiting room, his face pale and clammy. He looked right at me but didn't see me. He acted like he didn't see much of anything. Detective McCoy came around the corner, trying to console him, but it didn't do much good.

I looked at Cade, who was seated in the waiting room. "Where's Lily?"

He leaned over and whispered, "She's fine. The nurses put her in one of the spare beds. She doesn't have any idea what's going on."

I was grateful. She'd been through enough.

"Where is she?" I said.

"Four doors down on the right."

I found Lily's room and went inside, carefully closing the door behind me. She was curled up in the bed, asleep, a little stuffed unicorn tucked beneath her arm. If there was ever a time I wanted to shed tears for another human being, this was it. First her sister, and now her mother. I leaned over, kissing her on the cheek, and hoped she was still young enough to have a chance at a happy life.

When I returned to the waiting room, Cade was still there. "Look," he said, "about what happened earlier. I'm sorry I—"

I touched his arm. "Don't be. You were right."

He looked at me, puzzled.

I handed him the plastic case. He took it without saying anything, opened it, and then gripped it so tight, his knuckles changed color.

Through gritted teeth, he said, "Are you trying to help this case or sabotage it?"

I remained silent. He didn't.

"I've only known one other PI in my life, and they didn't take cases like you do. They did fluffy stuff like follow a woman's husband to see if he was cheatin', so I honestly don't know what's going on here. But if you think you can show up in my town, and disrespect all that my father has done for this family, I'll escort you back to Utah right now."

Maddie started to get up from her chair but I shook my head. I deserved every word. Cade had a right to feel the way he did. I was mad at myself. My heart was in the right place, but he didn't know me enough to understand who I was or what lengths I would go to in order to bring my client the justice they deserved. But right now wasn't the right time to explain it.

I tilted my head toward the front door and Maddie got up.

Cade shook his head.

"You don't have anything to say?"

I looked at him and whispered, "You're right, about everything, and I understand."

CHAPTER TWENTY-THREE

"So, that's it?" Maddie said. "You're packing up?"

It was morning, but my lack of sleep had made it seem like the past few days had all blended together somehow. I was packing, and for the first time in my life, I had no plan. No next move. Nothing. I didn't know why I was packing or what I was doing, but I had to do something. So I folded and organized. My current method of finding out what happened to the girls wasn't working. I needed a new one. I just didn't know what that was yet.

"I'm thinking of going home," I said.

"Why?"

"I need to clear my head."

"You're not quitting, are you?"

"Have I ever?" I said.

She shrugged.

"You're running away. It's what you do when things like this happen."

"That's not true."

"Of course it is. How long did it take you to return to

your hometown after you graduated? And even then, you've only been back twice: once for your aunt's funeral and just recently to solve a murder."

I flung a folded shirt into the suitcase, knowing I wouldn't be able to resist refolding it and lining it up with the others later. "Getting my head clear is not the same thing as running away. I don't bail on my cases. I don't need a lecture, Maddie. Not from you. Not today."

"Sloane, listen to me."

I folded a few more items and tossed them in.

Maddie stood in front of the suitcase, blocking me. "Will you stop for a minute and listen to me, please?"

I didn't want to, but I did anyway.

"You have the ability to push past all this," she said. "You've never backed down from a case before. Mrs. Tate is dead, Cade yelled at you, you haven't had any new leads in a few days, and you're under pressure. Part of it is probably because you're worried that when you find these girls, they won't be alive. I know it's hard. But you can't leave, not now."

"I'm not backing down. It's just...I've never had a case like this. It's not going anywhere. I feel like all I'm doing is letting people down. It's not who I am, Maddie."

"All you need is one break," she said. "Just one. Who knows? Maybe you've already set something in motion and you don't even know it yet."

"I honestly don't know where to go from here, Maddie," I said. "The children are ghosts in the wind. I have no idea how to find them—not even with the few new leads I have."

"You know why you're feeling this way, right?"

I shrugged. She continued.

"You haven't had any sleep, sweetie."

"I don't have time to sleep."

"Sure you do. Stop arranging your already-organized suitcase and lie down and rest for a few minutes. Clear your head. You'll thank me later."

"I don't know," I said.

Maddie flipped the lid of my suitcase closed. "It wasn't a suggestion. The Sloane I know doesn't back down from anything. So you're getting in that bed, and when you wake up, we can talk about where to go from here."

I took her advice, changed clothes, and snuggled up next to Lord Berkeley. It felt good to shut down, and this time, my body allowed it. When I woke several hours later, it was dark outside. Maddie was in the living room talking to someone. Her voice was low, and I couldn't make out what she was saying. I swept my hair back into a ponytail, pulled some pants on, and opened the door. To my surprise, Cade and Maddie were sitting at the table, chatting like they'd been friends for years. His snub from a few nights before at the bar seemed to have been long forgotten.

"Cade came by to see you," Maddie said. "But I've kept him a lot longer than he bargained for."

I looked at him. "Why?"

"We can discuss it tomorrow," he said, "when I take you to breakfast."

"Why don't we talk about whatever it is now?"

He glanced at his phone. "Because it's almost midnight,

I'm tired, and it can wait."

"How long have you been here?" I said.

"A couple hours."

Cade stood up and walked to the door.

"I might not be here in the morning," I said.

Maddie disregarded my comment and looked at Cade. "She'll see you in the morning. I'll make sure of it."

Cade nodded and opened the door, glancing at me before he went through it. "Night ladies."

CHAPTER TWENTY-FOUR

"When you said 'take you to breakfast,' I was thinking more along the lines of a diner, preferably one with a fireplace," I said.

Cade inhaled the cool mountain air and glanced around at the landscape surrounding us. "I can't imagine a more beautiful place than this. Besides, you got your very own fire right there."

He walked to the truck, lifted up the seat in the back, and pulled out a blanket. A minute later, it was wrapped around me.

"Don't you live in Park City?" he said. "I thought you'd be used to this kind of weather."

"I have no problem with winter. I just think it's a season best experienced indoors."

He shook his head.

"You know," he said. "You're just about the farthest thing from a country girl that I've ever met."

"And that's a bad thing?"

"To tell you the truth, I don't know what it is. You're

different."

"Different good or different bad?"

Instead of answering, he stirred some eggs in a thick black pan with a wooden spatula. The more he mixed them around, the more little black flecks of what appeared to be pieces of the pan mingled with the eggs until it resembled pepper. I tried not to make a face and instead wrapped the blanket tighter around me.

"So, what did you want to talk to me about?" I said.

He placed a finger in front of his lips and pointed across the meadow. "Do you see it?" he said in a hushed voice.

I saw nothing but trees and various kinds of sagebrush. "See what?"

"Here, look through my binoculars," he said, handing them to me.

I held them in front of my eyes. "I can't see a thing out of these; it's blurry."

He reached over, messing around with a knob in the middle. "You gotta adjust them a bit. Turn this dial until you can see clearly."

I tried what he suggested and gasped when I looked through the lenses again. The animal was far off, but viewing it through the binoculars made it seem closer. Too close. "That's the biggest deer I've ever seen!"

Cade smacked the side of his pants and laughed so hard I thought he'd fall off the log we were sitting on.

"What's so funny?" I said.

"That's no deer, woman. It's a bull elk."

Woman?

I shrugged.

"Deer, elk, same difference," I said.

"Actually, they're not the same at all. Elk are about three times bigger than deer, and their hair is yellow. A deer has brown hair."

The elk seemed to notice our presence, even though it didn't seem likely given our distance. It glanced around and slanted its head upward, making a noise Cade later explained as "bugling." Then it camouflaged itself inside a group of trees. I tried to find it again, but it was gone.

Cade scooted a little closer to me. "Would you look at that?"

The sunrise was among the prettiest I had ever seen and worth every moment I'd spent whining about the chilly temperatures. Just looking at it made me feel warmer.

"It's beautiful," I said.

Cade scooped the eggs onto two paper plates and handed one of the plates to me along with some hash browns that he'd mixed with pieces of bacon. I took a bite. They were surprisingly good.

"What do you think?" he said. "Does it meet your standards for breakfast?"

I nodded. He tossed a couple pieces of wood, stoking up the fire.

"I, uh, wanted to apologize for getting angry with you the other night," he said.

"You had every right. I would have done the same thing in your position."

"I was frustrated and tired, but not just at you," he said.

"Coming back hasn't been easy. The guys at the station make me feel like an outsider even though I grew up around here. And when the chief announced I'd be filling my father's position, it didn't go over well. I suppose I understand why, but I went to school with some of these guys, and they're being completely ignorant."

"Have you talked to them about it?"

"Tried to, but they haven't been very receptive," he said. "Chief Rollins and my dad go way back. They lived next door to each other when they was boys. Rollins is more like family to me than anything else. The other guys know it, think he's playing favorites. And maybe he is, but they don't know how qualified I am for the job or how many years I've been at it. They don't care, neither."

"In many ways, I know how you feel," I said. "It's not easy being a private investigator. I have a love/hate relationship going on with the police department in my town. It doesn't matter how much I've helped them over the years, they don't want me around. Not really. They probably feel like I make them look bad when I get something right that they couldn't."

"The truth is, I know a lot more about you than you think," he said.

I pulled my knees up in front of me, resting my chin on top. Then I repositioned the blanket. "Like what?"

"For starters, you've solved every case you've taken."

"How did you know? Did Maddie tell you?"

He shook his head.

"I looked into your background the day you met with Tate," he said. "Impressive. But what I don't understand is why'd you become a PI instead of a cop? You would have made detective by now."

"I don't like people," I said.

He raised a brow. "Care to explain yourself?"

"I don't possess the *works-well-with-others* gene. Never have. I like being on my own with no one to answer to but myself."

The look on his face let me know he could relate.

"The chief ran the paper Tate gave you."

"And?" I said.

"I'm not sure."

"About what?"

"The guys won't tell me if they got anything off of it. Right now, I'm not a member of their 'club,' but that's fine. If they're gonna continue actin' how they are, I don't wanna be."

"What about the envelope?" I said. "I'm guessing you handed it over too."

"Nope. Your friend Madison has it."

"Maddie? Why?"

The envelope had gone from Mr. and Mrs. Tate, to me, to Maddie, to Cade, and back to Maddie again. It would be a miracle if it produced anything useful at this point.

"I'll explain later, but right now, I was hopin' you'd tell me more about what you know about the case. You said a few things at Tate's house, and I have some questions."

I set my plate down and stood up. "Is that why you invited me out here, so you could get me to tell you what I know? I don't think so."

I considered walking back to the hotel, but I had no idea

where we were.

"Calm down, would ya? It's not what you think. I want us to work together."

I almost spit out the mouthful of eggs I had been chewing. "What? Still?"

"You heard me," he said.

"No one in law enforcement has ever wanted to work with me—not when they had another choice."

"Maybe they're intimidated because you're a woman, or maybe it's because you don't wear a badge," he said. "You're feisty as hell, but I don't scare easily. And besides, this is my dad's case. If anyone else is going to solve it besides him, it's going to be me."

There it was—the motivation behind why he wanted to work together. Cade knew the other guys were keeping things from him, doing all they could to make his job harder. They wanted him to fail. Either that or for him to reach a breaking point and leave, giving one of them his father's job. But Cade didn't strike me as the kind of guy who got pushed around. He wanted to find Savannah for his father, but he also had something to prove.

"Is that why Maddie has the envelope?" I said.

He nodded.

"No one besides the three of us knows you found it."

"And you're not concerned about—"

"I only care about one thing right now: finding out what happened to Savannah any way I can."

He sounded more like me all the time.

I told Cade about the other missing girl and her parents

who had also received a coloring page in the mail. I told him about my visit to Maybelle's Market and about meeting Todd, the only person to have seen the kidnapper. I told him about meeting Kris and Olivia's stepdad and the two old coots who thought Terrence was somehow involved in Olivia's abduction. Talking about it to someone else made me feel like I hadn't been such a failure, but it still wasn't much to go on.

Cade remained silent until I finished, and then he stuck his hand out. "You interested in tryin' this again?"

It seemed silly, but I shook his hand anyway.

"What now?" I said.

"Now you go back to the hotel and say goodbye to your friend. She said she needs to get back to her lab in order to process the envelope."

"And then?"

"Then you're going to meet Chief Rollins."

CHAPTER TWENTY-FIVE

I saw Maddie and Lord Berkeley off and joined Cade at his father's house. Cade wanted the meeting between the chief and me to take place outside of the police station, away from the scrutiny of the other members of the department, and I agreed. I hadn't wanted to meet the chief at all, but Cade insisted. He felt the new developments in the case needed to come from me. I wasn't so sure.

When I arrived, Chief Rollins was already there waiting. He said nothing to me when I entered the kitchen. Cade, his father, and the chief were huddled around the table arguing over a recent football game. Cade and his father smiled at me. The chief didn't even look up.

Cade's father didn't look well. His skin had yellowed even more than the last time I saw him, and he was nothing but skin and bones. I couldn't have been the only one to notice.

"Good, you're here," Cade said. "Chief Rollins, this is Sloane Monroe, the woman I was telling you about."

The chief still hadn't made any effort to look at me. I

wasn't sure what Cade thought would happen by throwing the two of us together, but it couldn't have been this. I sat down and thought about getting up and leaving, but I didn't. Cade looked at me like they were all waiting for me to say something, so I did.

"It's nice to meet you, Chief Rollins," I said.

He looked up, but he didn't smile. He squinted at me through a pair of glasses that were too big for his narrow face. They had the thickest lenses I'd ever seen. And they were dusty, like they hadn't been cleaned in ages. How he could see anything out of them was a mystery to me. The look on his face was neutral. I'd learned to read most people over the years, but I couldn't read him.

Without saying a word, the chief reached into the front pocket of his blue flannel shirt. He pulled out a small pad of paper and a pen, flipped to the first page of the pad, and snapped the top of the pen. He then looked back at me and twirled his hand around as if to say, 'Let's get on with it.'

Cade sensed the obvious tension in the room and said, "Why don't you tell him what you told me?"

The chief took notes as I relayed what little information I had that they didn't. He seemed to find what I said interesting, but not enough to ask any questions.

When I finished talking, he said, "Anything else?"

I shook my head.

"Good, you can go now," the chief said.

I could see this shocked Cade, from the look on his face, but I'd gotten used to it over the years. I didn't want to be there any more than the chief wanted me there.

Cade placed a hand on my arm before I could go anywhere. "Wait a minute."

The chief flicked his hand toward the door. "Let her go. We got what we needed."

"That's not why I asked her to come over," Cade said. "Sloane's good at what she does. She can help us. I don't see why she needs a badge. We all have the same goal here."

The words rolled off his tongue like he truly believed it, and maybe he did. But he was naïve to think he could put us in a room together and we'd get along.

"We don't need her," the chief said.

The sleep forced on me by Maddie had made me feel a lot more like myself again. And I didn't intend to stand there and listen to him talk like I was already gone.

"Of course you don't need me," I said. "You were doing a great job before I came along."

"Your sarcasm is unnecessary," the chief said. "As are you."

"Come on now, Harold," Cade's father said to the chief. "The girl's just trying to help. I'm grateful for what she's done."

Detective McCoy's eyes widened, and he gave me a look that said: *He's not always like this.*

"You have a missing girl, a dead mother, and a father who wants nothing to do with any of you," I said.

Cade and his father exchanged looks but said nothing. The chief didn't take his eyes off the notebook.

"Best if you went back to your hotel, packed your things, and were on your way," the chief said.

"I'm not leaving. I was hired to do a job, and I'll stay here until I see it through."

"Tate should be working with us, not with you," the chief said. "Why he sought you out in the first place baffles me. I'll make sure he corrects his mistake. He's only to deal with us now."

I leaned across the table until I was uncomfortably close to the chief's face. "Don't *ever* speak to me like I'm some second-class, second-rate person. You don't own me, and you don't own Mr. Tate."

"I never—"

"You can't even look me in the eye when you're talking to me," I said.

He closed the notebook and glared at me.

"You know nothing about me. Before I came here, you had no leads. I'm the one who tied the two cases together." I grabbed my bag and slung it over my shoulder. "I'm leaving. What I choose to do after I walk out the door is none of your business and none of your concern. And since you don't 'need me,' you don't have any reason to worry about it."

The chief opened his mouth to reply, but I held my finger out. "Don't."

When I got to the door, I heard Cade say, "I want her help on this. If it bothers you, no one else has to know. You brought me here. You said you trusted me. I need you to trust me now."

The chief replied, "It's not your decision."

"She stays, or I go," Cade said.

"You don't mean that, Cade," the chief said.

But somehow, I knew he did.

CHAPTER TWENTY-SIX

"I'm very sorry to bother you, Mr. Tate," I said. "Are you doing okay? How's Lily?"

Noah Tate stood in the doorway of his house looking like he hadn't had any sleep since the last time I saw him.

"Lily's with my sister."

"Is there anything I can do for you?" I said.

He shook his head.

"What about dinner?" I said. "Have you had anything to eat?"

"I can't hold anything down. I haven't been able to since…"

He hung his head, shielding his eyes with his hands.

"I've lost my wife, my daughter—there's nothing left. Nothing."

"You still have Lily," I said. "And you have me. I haven't given up on finding Savannah. No matter what the outcome, I intend to keep looking."

"I don't think I can take one more death in my family, Miss Monroe."

"But we don't know what's happened—"

"Please," he said, placing his weak hand on my shoulder, "I need to be alone for a while."

I left Mr. Tate's house and went to the store. He probably wouldn't eat anything I made anyway, but I'd never been good at sitting around and doing nothing. I bought everything I needed for my mother's homemade chicken soup. Whether he ate it or not would be up to him, but I was going to offer it either way.

When I got back to the hotel, Cade was waiting in the parking lot.

"What have you got there?" he said.

"I thought I'd make some soup."

"Okay?"

"It's for Mr. Tate."

"Need any help?" he said.

"No, but you can talk to me while I make it."

He took the bags I was carrying, and we went inside.

"I should have never put you in that position earlier," he said. "I had no idea he'd—"

"It's not the first time, and it won't be the last."

"I've never seen him act like that."

"Everyone is probably feeling a lot of pressure right now. I don't take it personally."

He sat down on the barstool. "It wasn't you though," he said.

"I appreciate you coming over here, but I'm fine. Don't worry about it."

"No, I mean, it really wasn't you."

"What do you mean?"

Cade folded one hand over the other, resting them on the ledge of the bar. "Feds are on their way. Since there's the possibility of one guy taking both kids, they're looking at both cases."

The feds coming in town didn't excuse the chief's callous behavior toward me.

"But they'll be working with police departments in both counties, right?"

He shook his head.

"The chief says they want all evidence turned over from both departments, ours and the one in Sublette County. It doesn't look like they want our help. They just want us to tell them what they need to know and then get out of the way. I'm not sure whether they'll see if there's anything they can do and then leave, or whether they're here indefinitely."

I thought about calling Giovanni's brother and using his FBI connections, but then I changed my mind. He was helping track down Daniela, and even if he wasn't, it was getting complicated enough. I didn't want either of them to get involved.

"We better work fast then," I said.

Cade smiled.

"What did you have in mind?"

"I have a question. I know there were no workers outside the day Savannah was abducted from the daycare, but what about the other child? Did she see anything?"

"Savannah was outside with her friend, Sierra Johnson, at

the time."

"How old is she?" I said.

"Five. And it hasn't been easy getting information out of her. I don't know if she even knows what she saw."

I chopped some carrots and threw them into the pot on the stove. In another pot I stirred the chicken. "Did your father interview Sierra?"

"He tried to, and so have I, but she didn't say much. Nothin' we could use."

"What did she say?"

"She told us the man drove a silver car, and she mentioned something about a black watch."

"Now that we know the kid at Maybelle's Market saw a silver Dodge Charger, maybe if we show a more specific picture to Sierra, she can identify it."

"Maybe."

"What are her parents like?" I said. "Do you think they'd let us talk to her again?"

He shrugged.

"Sierra lives with her mother. They're divorced. She's very protective of her daughter."

"Maybe if I saw her alone," I said. "The feds will question everyone. They'll start from the beginning and cover all their bases. We need to get to Sierra before they do. After that, I probably won't be able to talk to her or anyone else without them knowing it."

"I don't like the idea of you seeing her without me."

"You said you wanted my help with this, and I know you meant together, but I'm good at talking to people, especially women. Whatever I find out, I'll share it with you."

It came down to a matter of trust, but I knew it wouldn't be easy for him to put his confidence in me until I had proven myself. This would give me the opportunity.

I removed the chicken from the stove, shredded it, and added it to the pot of vegetables and broth. "When this is done, I need to run it over to Mr. Tate's house."

"I can do it for you."

"I don't mind taking it to him," I said.

"I'll be on my way home anyway. I can just drop it off."

"When I stopped by earlier, he wasn't in the mood for company. He actually asked me to leave him alone for a while."

"I'll set it on the doorstep, ring the doorbell, and leave."

I poured some of the soup into a container, put it in a bag, and handed it to Cade. He leaned in, but instead of taking the soup, he said, "You've got an eyelash on your…"

He swept the lash from my eye with his finger but then remained there, gazing at me, our faces inches apart. I tried not to make assumptions. Up until that moment, he'd seemed more like a *pain-in-the-butt* brother than anything else. Cade remained there for several seconds, as if gauging my reaction. I was too shocked to move. He placed his hand over mine on the bag and held it there.

"I, ahh, guess you should get this to him while it's still hot," I said.

He took the bag. "See you tomorrow."

CHAPTER TWENTY-SEVEN

My phone rang to a number I didn't recognize.

"Miss Monroe?"

"Who's this?" I said.

"Jenny. Do you remember me?"

"From Maybelle's Market?" I said.

"Yes. I thought I should tell you, Todd went in and talked to the police."

I knew that already, but I appreciated the call anyway.

"How did it go?" I said.

"They had him sit down with one of those people who draw things."

"A sketch artist?"

"Yes. He did the best he could. They released the sketch; it's all over town. But the guy would be long gone by now, so I don't really know what they think is going to happen."

"Jenny, could you email me a copy of it?" I said.

"Sure."

"How's Todd doing?"

"All right. No one knows it was him. They just know

someone came forward."

I was glad to hear it, but with the feds coming, all that was all about to change. I only hoped Todd wouldn't suffer too much for it. I ended the call with Jenny and answered another one from Giovanni.

"Have you found your sister yet?" I said.

"Last night."

He sounded relieved. I was too.

"How is she?" I said.

"In shock, but she's alive."

"Did anything *happen* to her?"

"From what we understand, she was treated quite well." He paused. "When are you coming back? I want to see you."

"I don't know yet," I said. "Did you find the men who took her?"

He was quiet for a moment before responding.

"Giovanni, are you there?" I said.

"We took care of everything. I'll be home tomorrow."

It was just like usual. I asked questions, but only received vague answers. Our relationship had always been one-sided. I recognized that, but I thought in time, it could change, that he'd open up to me, like I had tried to do with him. Funny thing about trying to *change* a person—it never worked.

"I'd like to know more about what happened," I said.

"And you will, but let's talk about it later. Right now, I just want you here with me. Tell me about the case you're working on."

Ahh, the switch. Giovanni had mastered changing the subject whenever it suited him, which was every time I asked him something he considered too intimate to reveal. If I pushed him, I would still get nothing, and I knew it.

I told Giovanni about the two missing girls, but left most of the details out. He'd been through a grueling ordeal with his sister, and I wanted him to focus on her for the time being.

"Tell me what I can do to help you," he said when I'd finished.

"I appreciate it, but I'm fine."

"If you need anything, just call."

"I will."

I ended the call and checked my email for the flyer Jenny sent. It was just like I expected. The mind is a great thing, but in time, even the most vivid memories fade. Two years is long enough for important details to be forgotten. The sketch revealed little in the way of a unique face. There was nothing in the sketch that made the man stand out in any way. He had a square-shaped head, a defined jawline, stubble that hadn't been shaved in a day or two, and oval-shaped sunglasses. He looked like a cop with a five o'clock shadow. Another dead end.

CHAPTER TWENTY-EIGHT

Cade told me I could find Mrs. Johnson at home after three o'clock, so I arrived just after, hoping she was already there. A green Toyota of some kind was parked out front, making me optimistic.

I knocked on the door a few times and moments later it opened.

"Can I help you?"

Sierra's mother had a petite frame and couldn't have been much taller than about five foot two. She had a milky white face and long, straight blond hair that was so light, it was almost white in color. She didn't look like a woman who was highly stressed, although as a single mom, she undoubtedly was on occasion.

"My name is Sloane," I said. "I'm a friend of the Tates. I wondered if I could talk to you for a few minutes.

"What about?"

"Mr. Tate has hired me to investigate Savannah's disappearance, and I was hoping I could get your permission to spend a few minutes with Sierra."

"You're very straightforward, Ms. Monroe."

"In my experience, I've found it's best to be honest from the get-go," I said.

"I decided a few months ago that it was too hard on Sierra to speak to the police. She gets very scared when they question her, no matter how nice they are. I'm sorry, but I can't help you."

"Mrs. Tate is dead," I said.

She placed a hand over her chest.

"What—when?"

"It happened a couple nights ago."

She frowned.

"I'm very sorry. I had no idea. Please tell Noah to let me know if he needs anything."

I nodded, and she took a step back, preparing to close the door.

"Some new information has surfaced over the past week," I said.

"I'm glad. I hope you find Savannah. I really do. She was Sierra's best friend. They played together almost every day, even when they weren't at school."

No matter how pleasant she appeared, her patience was wearing thin.

"I know you want to spare Sierra from thinking about what happened that day," I said quickly, "but it's just going to get worse."

"What do you mean?"

"The FBI is getting involved for reasons I can't really go into right now, but once they get here, you won't have a choice. Your daughter will have to speak to them, no matter how you feel. I'm not saying this to be rude. I just thought you should know."

"I don't understand. She's already met with Detective McCoy and his son a few times. There isn't any reason to put her through it all again."

"The FBI will be conducting its own investigation," I said. "Whatever has happened in the past will be thrown out. From what I've been told, they plan on building their own case."

She pulled the door back a few inches and contemplated what to do next. "I don't want her to go through it all again. Can you stop it from happening?"

It would have been easy to lie to her and make a deal so I could get what I needed, but I wouldn't have felt right about deceiving her.

"I honestly don't know. I can promise you this— whatever I find out today I will share with Cade McCoy, and he will do everything he can to help you. But if you want my honest opinion, they'll come anyway."

"What should I do?"

"Is there somewhere you could take Sierra for a few days or send her?" I said. "They'll have plenty to do when they first get here, so that might take the attention off Sierra and put it somewhere else."

"I don't know. I suppose."

"I'm not telling you to avoid the FBI or not to work with them. I would never do that. But maybe if you spoke to them first, without Sierra here, you could appeal to them as a mother. It wouldn't hurt to explain your feelings. Maybe they'll take it under consideration."

"I appreciate your help," she said.

I didn't want to push by asking her to speak with her daughter one last time, so I didn't. In a situation like this, it all came down to respect.

I turned.

"Enjoy the rest of your day."

Hold on a minute," she said. "I'll let you speak to Sierra, but just for a few minutes, and only if she is receptive to you. If she isn't, please don't force her."

"I will be as sensitive and as quick as I can," I said.

She flattened her hand. "Wait here."

Mrs. Johnson returned a few minutes later and invited me in. "I'd like to sit in while you talk with her."

"I wouldn't have it any other way," I said.

Sierra sat nervously on the living room sofa, looping her fingers around the edge of a piece of fabric from the outfit she was wearing.

"I like your dress," I said when I walked into the room. "It's very pretty."

She looked at her mother but not at me. When talking to children Sierra's age in the past, I found their attention span was minimal. I needed to keep the conversation brief. It was best to ask specific questions, making it easy for her to answer. She needed simplicity so she didn't become confused.

I sat down on a chair next to the sofa, giving Sierra the space she needed.

"I'm trying to find your friend, Savannah," I said.

Sierra looked over at me. "Do you know where she is?"

"Not yet," I said. "I was hoping you could help me."

She looked at her mom again and frowned.

"But I don't know where she is."

"I saw Lily the other day. We made macaroni and cheese together. She seems pretty lonely without her sister to play with."

Sierra's face changed. I knew she was listening to me, but she still wasn't ready to talk. Her mother looked at me and nodded, letting me know it was okay to continue.

"Someone told me a man came to the daycare, and that when he left, he took her with him. I want to find the man so I can ask him to give her back, but I don't know what he looks like. Can you help me?"

Sierra's mother put her arm around her daughter. "It's okay, honey. This nice lady is my friend."

Sierra nodded and crossed her legs under her dress.

"Did you see the man who took Savannah?" I said.

She bobbed her shoulders up and down.

"I don't know."

Ms. Johnson said, "She never looked at his face."

I imagined since he was a stranger, Sierra had been too frightened. Maybe that's why she'd noticed other things, like the watch and the color of the car.

"If I show you a few pictures, do you think you could tell me if it's the car you saw the man driving?"

She thought about it.

"Okay."

I pulled some photos out of my purse that I had printed earlier that morning. The first was a Ford Mustang. "Is this one it?"

She shook her head.

Next I tried a Chevrolet Camaro. She scooted to the edge of the sofa and looked harder at it. Again, she shook her head.

Now that I had her attention, I held the picture of the Dodge Charger in front of her. "What about this one?"

As soon as she saw it, she jerked back. I folded the picture and put it away. "Was that the car you saw?"

She nodded.

The watch would be harder for her to identify, and I questioned its significance. I hadn't brought any photos, but I wore one to see if it triggered anything.

"Do you have a watch?" I said.

She didn't budge.

"Lily has one," I said. "She was wearing it the last time I saw her. It's pink and has a princess head on it. She pushes a button and it flips open. Mine's not fun like Lily's. But it's special. My grandpa gave it to me."

Sierra hopped off the sofa and dashed down the hall. I looked at her mother. "Is she okay? I hope I haven't said anything to upset her."

Ms. Johnson said, "I don't know. Let me go see if I can—"

Before she could finish her sentence, Sierra returned, holding her balled hand out in front of me. She unrolled her fingers and revealed a red and pink watch. It had hearts all over it. In the center of the dial it said 'Sierra.'

"My grandpa gave me one, too," Sierra said. "He said it has lots of hearts 'cuz that's how much he loves me."

"It's beautiful," I said. "Your grandpa must love you very

much."

She smiled. "He does. He tells me every day." She looked at the watch I was wearing. "Why do you wear your watch right there?"

"I'm not sure what you mean. How should I wear it?"

Sierra put her hand on my upper arm. "Grownups are supposed to wear them 'right here.'"

I wondered if she was tired of talking and was playing some kind of game with me. I played along to see. "Who would wear a watch way up there?"

"The bad man," she said.

Ms. Johnson looked at me, confused. "I'm sorry. I don't know what she's talking about. I think she's done for today."

"Wait a minute," I said. "I don't think she's joking. Sierra, what did it look like?"

She made a face like she was trying to remember. "He didn't know what time it was."

"Why?"

"It was broken, silly."

It clicked, and I finally understood what she was trying to say. "Was it a tattoo?"

Sierra looked at her mother. "What's a tact-too?"

"Did it look like my watch or did it look like a picture?" I said.

"He needed to color it."

"Ms. Johnson, do you have a piece of paper and a pen?" I said.

Although startled, she got the items for me.

"I'm not very good at drawing," I said, "but you tell me if

this is what you saw?"

I drew a watch that had numbers but no hands pointing to the time. "Did it look like this?"

She nodded and jumped up and down. "Yay! Will you find Savannah now?"

I looked down at her hopeful face, trying to remember what it felt like to be an innocent child, free from the harsh realities of life.

I patted her on the shoulder. "I will do my best."

Sierra looked at her mother. "Mommy, can I go play now?"

Ms. Johnson looked at me, hoping I was finished. I nodded.

Once Sierra was out of earshot, her mother said, "What Sierra told you, is it a big deal?"

"It could be. I'm not sure yet."

We walked to the door and I thanked her again. I was just about to get in my car when Sierra came running up behind me yelling, "Wait, give her this!"

She thrust a stuffed teddy bear into my hands. "This is Mr. Fluffy. He'll keep her safe."

"You are a good friend, Sierra," I said. "I'm sure Savannah misses you very much."

I waved goodbye and drove away. Without even knowing it, a five-year-old girl had just changed everything.

CHAPTER TWENTY-NINE

I tried Cade on his cell phone, but he didn't answer. Since I knew he was staying with his father until he made other living arrangements, I tried Detective McCoy's house first. A teenage girl answered the door with a greeting of, "Yeah?"

"Is Cade here?" I said.

"Who are you?"

"Someone he works with."

"Name?"

"Sloane," I said.

She clenched each side of the door jamb with her hands, blocking the entrance to the house. The oversized t-shirt she was wearing barely covered her bottom. She didn't seem to care. And with a body like hers, I could see why.

"What do you want?" she snapped.

"I'm here to see Cade," I said, again. "Is he here?"

She shrugged.

"Maybe."

"Let's try this another way," I said. "Are you his daughter?"

She laughed.

"Let's not try this at all. We're not 'friends,'" she said, doing air quotes with her fingers. "What do you want with my dad?"

"We're working on a case together," I said.

She rolled her eyes.

"I heard."

In many ways, teenagers were scarier to me than the criminals I pursued for a living. I understood criminals, what made them tick, why they did the things they did. But hormone-driven, pimply-faced kids? I didn't have a clue. The disrespectful ones grated on my nerves. Standing in front of Cade's daughter, I could see she had been enabled in her life, a bit too much from the looks of it. Others may have put up with her *less-than-civil* attitude, but she wouldn't get away with it—not with me.

"I don't know what I've done to piss you off," I said, "but I'm not going to stand here and go the rounds with you. Is your dad here, or isn't he?"

She scoffed.

"My dad is not available."

"To what—talk to me?" I said.

"To date you."

"We work together. What part of that don't you understand?"

"Puh-lease," she said. "I'm not some little kid you can stand here and lie to, so don't, okay?"

"Where did you get the idea that we were more than friends?" I said.

"He talks about you all the time. To my grandpa, to my grandma—it's disgusting."

"Shelby!"

Cade raced down the stairs. Upon seeing her father, Shelby suddenly learned how to smile while sucking up at the same time.

"What dad? We were just talking," she said. "Weren't we, Sloane?"

"Your daughter has a wild imagination," I said.

He pointed toward some rooms down the hall and said, "Move it, now."

She hung her head and slumped down the hall.

"I hope Shelby—"

"She didn't," I said. "Don't worry about it."

He waved his hand for me to follow him downstairs. I did.

The lower part of Detective McCoy's house was decorated in what I could only assume was typical Wyoming man-cave style, though I hadn't seen enough houses in the state to assess it properly. Taxidermy was everywhere. A grizzly bear stood in the corner of the room with his mouth wide open. His razor-sharp claws angled toward me, ready to attack. On a cut-out shelf in the wall, a wolf held his head high. I waited for the howling sound effects to start, but none did. I looked around. The rest of the room contained various mounted heads, some from animals I never knew existed.

"Are you okay being down here?" Cade said.

"It's a little different. I think I can manage."

"No hunters in your family?"

"Well, I never had a brother, and my dad didn't have many hobbies. Is your daughter all right?"

"Shelby's a teenager," he said. "I'm not sure she's ever 'all right.'"

"She didn't seem too thrilled we were working together."

He raised a brow.

"What did she say to you?"

"Not much—but I did get a 'keep away' vibe from her. I'm sure she's just going through a lot right now."

"Sounds like you've been talking to my dad," he said.

"He mentioned a few things to me."

"Him too?"

"It wasn't much. I'm sorry, I shouldn't have said anything."

Cade sat down. "Don't be sorry. My dad's got a lot on his mind right now. Besides, it don't matter to me if he told you. It's not a secret. My wife left. I've moved on."

"I'm not sure your daughter has."

"She's unhappy either way—I just do the best I can with her. She might not realize it right now, but being here around my parents is helping her deal with everything. I hope one day she'll realize it instead of hating me for bringing her here."

"She didn't want to move?"

"She misses her deadbeat boyfriend, which is one more reason we needed a change in scenery."

"Sounds like you're a great father."

He smiled and pointed at my hands. "What have you got there?"

I unfolded my less-than-stellar drawing. "Have you seen a tattoo like this before?"

He curled his fingers toward him. I handed the drawing over. "You draw this?"

"We all have our qualities," I said. "Drawing isn't one of mine."

He winked.

"I can tell," he said.

"Do you know what it is?"

"Do you?" he said.

I nodded.

"Then you know where guys get these?" he said.

"Yeah, in prison."

"Do you know what it means?"

"I think so," I said. "It's a prison tattoo. A clock with no hands symbolizes the person is serving time, usually a lot of it, and that the time that ticks by is meaningless."

"That's why it doesn't have any hands," he said, "because time doesn't matter when you're serving a long sentence."

"Sierra Johnson told me the man who took Savannah had this tattoo on his upper arm."

Cade shook his head and smiled. "Well, I'll be damned."

Cade used his connections to see if he could get a list of released inmates over the past several years that had a tattoo of a clock on their upper arm. He also talked them into sending along corresponding photos. The thought of getting the actual name of the guy made me nervous, but in a good way. It felt great to finally have a solid lead. I just hoped it went somewhere.

I called Maddie and gave her the news.

"I was just about to call you," she said.

"Did you get anywhere with the envelope?"

"Lots of places after I dealt with all the prints on the outside of it. Do you have any idea how many people have touched this thing?"

"I probably don't want to know."

"Trust me," she said. "You don't. The outside of it was a mess. Too many prints, all over the place. I've got prints on top of prints, smudged prints, partial prints. You get the idea."

"So, you didn't get anything?"

She popped a bubble into the phone. "I did."

Maddie was biding her time, which meant she had good news.

"I lifted a perfect print from the inside, right under the place a person would lick and stick, except for whoever sealed this thing, didn't do it very well. It was only sticky in the center, you know, the pointy part on the back. The beauty of it is, the only people to touch the inside were Mr. and Mrs. Tate and the sender of the letter."

"Do you have a name?" I said.

"Not yet. Since I don't know who this print belongs to, I have to run it through the database. Hopefully we'll get a hit."

"How long will it take?" I said.

"We're running it now. How are things on your end?"

I filled her in on the recent developments thinking she'd have a lot to say, but when I finished, she didn't say anything. She was quiet. Too quiet. It was almost like she was no longer on the line, but the seconds ticked by on the front of my phone. For whatever reason, she didn't seem to be listening.

"Are you still there?" I said.

"Umm, yeah. Can you hold on a minute? One of my guys is waving me over."

I held for a minute, and then two, until I considered hanging up and letting her call me back. But then I heard her voice in the background. It was slightly muffled, but it was Maddie's voice all the same. She was talking to someone.

She said, "Are you sure?"

The other person responded, "One hundred percent."

"Sloane," she said, breathing heavily into the phone, "we've got a match."

CHAPTER THIRTY

Searching the database for a latent print, even an excellent specimen like the one Maddie found inside the envelope, was tricky. Not everyone had fingerprints that were searchable. Aside from a man or a woman who had committed some type of crime, the database contained prints from people like child-care workers, law enforcement, people who carried concealed weapons, teachers, and security-type workers, among others. And that was just one hurdle. Laws varied by state, making it even harder in some cases to access specific kinds of files.

Maddie struck fingerprint gold, matching the print she found to a teacher, a female by the name of Regina Kent. This matched my theory that someone sent the letters to both Olivia and Savannah's parents out of guilt and remorse, making a woman the most likely candidate. Now I just needed to know if I was right about why she'd done it. Did she have Olivia and Savannah? And was the man who took both girls her husband or someone else she was close to?

It didn't take long for me to get one of my answers. Cade did some digging and came up with some information on

Regina Kent. She was married to Bradley Kent, a retired surgeon twenty years her senior. His age made it less than likely that he was the one who'd kidnapped the two girls. According to our eyewitness, Todd, the man he saw in front of Maybelle's Market looked like he was in his mid-to-late forties. Even if Todd was off by a decade, Bradley Kent was pushing sixty. Even a teenage boy with a fleeting memory couldn't have been off by that much.

Cade learned Regina Kent had been a school teacher until three years earlier. According to the principal of the school, she walked in one day in the middle of the year and quit without any warning. I wondered why, but soon I would have the answer to my question. Cade had an address, and it wasn't even fifteen miles away.

I waited outside of the hotel for Cade to pick me up. I couldn't help but reflect on what a difference a few days made. Four nights earlier, seeing Cade in his Dodge Ram sent a pulsating wave of nerves throughout my body, and now I was anticipating his arrival. Even though he'd said we would work together on this case, I never expected him to keep his word, so I was astounded when he asked me to tag along. The feds were flying in the next morning. If we were going to find something on our own, we had to be quick.

Cade pulled to a stop next to me and popped the passenger-side door open. He had one hand on the wheel and the other stretched out across the top of the seat. I thought he'd move it when I got in, but he didn't.

A thin toothpick hung out of his mouth again. He looked at me and smiled. It was one of those casual smiles a person gives to another person when they've become comfortable in the relationship. But I was nowhere near being able to reciprocate.

"Why are you sitting like that?" he said.

"Like what?"

"Like you're going steady with the door."

"Well, your arm is in my way."

"I'm not even touching you, woman," he said. "Relax."

He moved his hand, resting it on his thigh.

"Is that what you call every female you meet?"

He laughed.

"What, *woman*?"

I nodded. He winked.

"Only the ones I like."

I didn't dare look over. I wasn't sure whether he was serious or just messing around. And I didn't want to know— at least, that's what I told myself. Cade leaned over and turned the volume up on the radio. Some guy singing what sounded like a mix of country and hard rock blared through the speakers.

"Who is he—and what is he?" I said.

"The singer? Brantley Gilbert. You like it?"

I reached over, turning it back down. "Not really."

Cade cranked it back up. "Give it a minute. It will grow on you."

Country music rarely did anything for me, but I had to admit, the song was catchy. When it was over, Cade pushed a button and shut the radio off.

"There's something I haven't told you about the Kents," he

said.

"What is it?"

"They had two children," he said.

"Had?"

"Yep, both dead," he said.

"Let me guess, girls?"

Cade nodded.

I swallowed—hard.

"Do you have any water?" I said.

Cade reached under the seat and handed me a can of soda. "Here, drink this."

"No thanks. I don't drink soda."

He gently tossed it into my lap. "Stop complaining, and just drink it."

I popped the top on the can and took a few sips. I had to admit, it tasted good.

"What happened to their children?" I said.

"I talked to the principal at the school Regina Kent worked at. He told me some years back, Regina decided to visit her parents in Utah over the holidays. Bradley couldn't go; he had too many patients to see. Regina packed up the car and got the kids ready, but by the time they left, it was almost midnight. They were tired, so she told the kids they could sleep in the car."

"Let me guess," I said. "She let them lay down, no seatbelts."

He nodded and continued.

"It started snowing, the roads were slick, and Regina thought about heading back home, but she was more than halfway to Utah already. She woke the girls and told them to put their seatbelts on. In the process, she turned around. They were hit head-on by a semi-truck on the highway. The car rolled several times. By the time the ambulance was on the scene, both girls were dead. Regina was the only survivor."

The idea of a child dying right in front of his parents was surreal to me.

"I think I'd rather not have a child at all than to face one of my kids dying before me. The guilt she felt must have been excruciating."

"I'm sure Regina felt the same way," he said. "After the accident, she quit her job and went into hiding, completely cutting herself off from society. Before the accident, she was well known around here. And after, she was well-known, but for an entirely different reason. People in town say she went crazy."

CHAPTER THIRTY-ONE

In the wake of her children's deaths, Regina Kent became a recluse, never going out for anything. The people in town hadn't seen her in years. Everyone assumed she'd locked herself inside of her house, deciding she was too fragile to ever venture out into the public eye again. Bradley Kent took a few weeks off after the children died and then resumed his practice. A year later, he retired. By that time he'd become somewhat of an enigma, at times displaying heartfelt emotions over his children, and at other times, behaving like they'd never existed at all. The principal told Cade he'd seen Bradley around from time to time, but never with Regina.

The Kents lived on a twenty-acre ranch surrounded by sprawling hills as far as the eye could see. White fencing that appeared to be made of some type of heavy-duty plastic lined the property on all sides. A team of horses stood like statues in the pasture, not moving, but gazing in our direction, curious about who we were and what we were doing there.

The multi-level house sat a few acres behind a long, paved driveway. It was a cabin, but not like any cabin I'd ever seen before. The logs were knotty and dark, and bigger than any I'd ever seen before.

We parked at the end of the drive, walked up to the door, and knocked. All was quiet. Two oversized whiskey barrels were positioned on both sides of the door. Potted plants had been inside of them at one time, but now, only a few shriveled up stems remained. There were cobwebs on everything: the windows, the corners of the door, and even between the wood railings on the wraparound porch.

"There's no one here," I said. "I thought Regina never left the house?"

Cade raised his shoulders. "I thought so too."

"Except for the horses, it doesn't look like anyone has lived here for a while."

Cade walked around the house, looking for a possible point of entry, but everything had been sealed up tight.

"That's a shame," I said.

"So's this," Cade said.

A rock whizzed by my head, creating a grapefruit-sized hole when it crashed through the front window.

Cade grinned.

"Would you look at that? Someone has vandalized this house. We'd better go inside and investigate."

To make a small hole even bigger, Cade used a stick to break up the hole in the window until it was big enough for him to step through. Then he unlocked and opened the front door.

I'd never been around a member of law enforcement who'd acted like Cade before, so for a minute, I just stood there.

"Was you plannin' on just standin' there, or you gonna come in sometime?" Cade patted me on my shoulder. "It's going to be okay. No one's here."

And because no one else lived next to them, there was a good chance we wouldn't see any visitors anytime soon.

"I'll take the main level, and you check upstairs," he said.

The area upstairs was nothing but a couple of bedrooms, a bonus room used as another living room, and a bathroom. The hallway was lined with various photos of wildlife that looked like they'd been taken in the area. In one photo, the Kent girls were sitting on two of the horses. In another, the girls and their parents stood outside a small house surrounded on all sides by masses of mature pine trees. The girls looked happy.

I entered the first bedroom. It was a child's room decorated in pink and grey and filled with everything but the child. It looked like it had been preserved just the way it had been left the last day she was alive. A shirt and a pair of pants were on the floor, indicating she had changed. A bathroom towel hung behind the door. I didn't want to touch anything for fear of altering the time-capsule state.

I found the same type of thing in the next room. A dollhouse sat in the corner. Inside, a family of dolls was positioned at the table. Wooden pieces of food were set in front of the man and the woman. The room didn't seem as mature as the other one. I looked in the closet. The clothes on the hangers were a size-four toddler. Four. The same age Savannah was when she was taken.

I went back into the other room, putting my sweater over my hands so I wouldn't leave any prints behind. I opened the door to the closet. I pulled out a dress. It was a size six. I looked at some others. There were a few sevens, but the majority of the closet contained size six. The same age as Olivia.

I pressed one of the dresses against my chest and thought about what a coincidence it was that the Kent girls were the same ages when they were alive as Olivia and Savannah when they were abducted. I breathed deeply, but it felt like the air I ingested wasn't circulating right. I sprinted to the stairwell and looked down.

"Cade?"

He was in the kitchen sorting through some drawers. He stopped and looked up at me. "What's wrong?"

I ran, skipping stairs to get to him. "I've figured out the connection between the Kents and the girls."

My theory was that the Kent girls had been replaced after their untimely deaths. At first Cade dismissed it, thinking my suggestion was nothing more than a fluke. But I didn't care what he thought. In all my years as a private investigator, I'd come to realize life didn't always have to make perfect sense.

"Do you have any idea how many married couples want to have children, and when they start trying, they find out they're infertile?" I said.

"It doesn't mean you're right about what happened to Olivia and Savannah."

It didn't mean I was wrong, either.

"Over six million," I said.

"Yeah, but don't most of them decide to adopt?"

"Do you think couples can just walk into an adoption center, fill out a form, flip through an album, and pick out their baby?"

He shrugged.

"Maybe it's hard here, in the US, but that's why most people adopt foreign babies."

"Most people aren't celebrities, Cade. Do you have any idea how long it takes?"

"Even with a couple who can have babies, it doesn't happen instantly. Sometimes it takes months for a woman to get pregnant. Then there's nine months of waitin' before it comes out. I should know."

"Lucky you," I said.

"What's that supposed to mean?"

"Nothing," I said.

He grabbed my wrist. Not hard, but enough to show me he was serious. "It's not nothin'. What aren't you saying?"

"It doesn't matter—it doesn't have anything to do with the case."

"I don't care—tell me. I'm not lettin' go 'til you do."

I was perfectly capable of freeing myself from the hold he had on me, but I didn't bother.

In a hushed voice I said, "I tried to have a baby once."

I wasn't sure he heard me, until he let go.

Cade took a step back. He looked at anything other than me, like if he locked eyes with me in that moment, he'd have to deal with female waterworks, but he was wrong.

"I don't want to talk about it," I said. "It was a long time ago. It's no big deal."

Cade pulled a chair out from under the table and gestured toward it. I sat down. He did the same. He tried to take my hand in his, but I pulled back. It didn't dissuade him.

"I, uh, appreciate you sharin' something so personal with me. I know it's not easy for you—I can tell."

I felt a sudden sensation of vertigo. I closed my eyes. When I opened them again, Cade had leaned closer to me, hovering a few inches over my face.

"What are you—"

"I came fifty percent of the way," he said. "This is the part where you come the other fifty."

I didn't know what to say. I knew what I *should* have said, but I hesitated. I didn't know why.

He wrapped his fingers around my chin, attempting to guide me the rest of the way. "I'm going to kiss you now."

"Cade…I…I'm in a relationship with someone."

He released me. "Of course you are. I'm sorry. I shouldn't have—"

"Don't be. I think you're great."

"No woman has ever, and I mean not *ever*, described me as *great* before," he said. "I don't even know what that means."

"It means I really like working with you."

"The feelin' is mutual, but I suppose you already—aww, hell. Can we change the subject? I know you weren't finished with what you were sayin' before, so I'm just going to sit here and try to keep an open mind."

I nodded, grateful for the reprieve.

"Many couples have a hard time adopting, and when that happens, some people turn to other methods. With the Internet so accessible these days, you can find other options."

"Such as?" he said. "I'm guessin' you're not gonna tell me about somethin' that's legal."

"Correct. There are illegal agencies that will help people get babies. Not adoption agencies—it's more along the lines of human trafficking. Do you know much about it?"

He tilted his head to the side. "A bit."

"There are a couple of ways it usually happens. Some agencies kidnap children and offer them up for sale to the highest bidder, or they kidnap the children until reward money is offered and then return them. At other agencies, a person is hired to find a certain type of child. The person who hires the agency can request anything they want—any age, a boy or a girl, it doesn't matter. Nothing is out of their reach."

He shook his head in disbelief.

"Do you really think the Kents paid someone to replace their children?"

"I do."

CHAPTER THIRTY-TWO

If the girls had been kidnapped to be raised by someone else, odds were they might still be alive. Getting kidnapped for any other reason besides a marital spat between divorcees meant the girls were most likely dead, and I had to believe they were still out there somewhere, alive and waiting for someone to find them.

Although it was getting late, Cade and I hadn't left the house yet. Both of us reasoned that if we picked the Kents' house apart a little longer, maybe we'd come up with some evidence that would lead us to Mr. and Mrs. Kent. But the house was clean. I was about to suggest we leave when I noticed headlights beaming through the window in the front of the house. Since we had already trespassed, and the vehicle had come to a stop and turned its lights off, we decided to face whoever it was rather than try and make a quick getaway.

A person exited the vehicle and I heard the sound of a rifle being prepped for use. Cade tried to push me behind the wall of the hallway with one hand, but I grabbed hold of him first, pulling him with me. We both drew our weapons.

"How long you been packin' that around?" Cade whispered.

"Don't act like you haven't seen it," I said. "You pat people down for a living."

"Haven't frisked you yet."

Even though he had his back to me, I knew he was smiling. I could tell by the sarcasm in his voice.

The front door opened, heavy footsteps followed, stomping their way across the floor.

"Who's there?" a male voice said.

Neither of us spoke.

"You're on private property," the voice said.

He sounded young, like he'd passed puberty, but not with an A.

"Where's the sign?" I said.

"What?" the boy said.

"I didn't see a sign stating this is private property."

"Well, it is," the boy said.

"How do I know you're the one who isn't trespassing then?"

There was a pause, like he couldn't come up with a logical answer.

"I'm armed," he said.

"That makes two of us," I said.

"Three," Cade said.

"Wait—there are two of you?" he said.

The boy could count, and he was nervous, which was good—as long as we could get him to put the rifle down. We were finally getting somewhere, just a lot slower than I'd imagined.

"I'm going to save you some time," I said. "We'll tell you who we are, and then you're going to tell us who you are."

"How will I know you're not lying?" he said.

"Oh, for goodness sake," I said to Cade. "Show the kid your badge before he does something stupid."

"I'm going to show you my badge now," Cade yelled loud enough for the entire neighborhood to hear. "Don't shoot my hand off or anything you'll live to regret." Cade took out his badge, edging his hand around the corner of the wall. "My name is Cade McCoy, and my partner here is Sloane Monroe."

Partner?

"We're detectives," Cade said. "Your turn."

He hesitated and then said, "My name is Henry."

"You have a last name Henry?" Cade said.

"Kent."

"How are you related to the owners of this house?" Cade said.

"Brad is my uncle."

"Bradley Kent?" Cade said.

"Yes."

"Henry, I want you to put down the rifle and slide it across the floor," Cade said.

"Right now?"

"Yes, now. Do you want me to count it out for you?" Cade said.

I heard the sound of a rifle being placed on the floor. Once it slid across, Cade walked around the corner and then signaled for me to do the same. The kid had his hands up and a look on his face like he wasn't sure what to expect next.

"Relax," I said.

"Am I in trouble?"

I shook my head.

"We're here because of the break in," I said.

"The what?"

I pointed at the window. The kid turned around and looked at it and then back at me, looking both convinced and relieved.

"Why are *you* here?" I said.

"I take care of my uncle's horses."

"Isn't it a little late in the day?" I said.

Cade looked at me like I had no idea what I was talking about.

"There are lights in the barn," the kid said. "I'm not here this late every night. I had a date."

"Where's your uncle?" I said.

"I don't know."

"You expect me to believe you tend his horses, and probably get paid for it too, but you don't know where he is?"

"He asked me if I could take care of them while he was gone."

"Gone where?" I said.

"Thailand." The way he said it sounded like he didn't believe it himself.

"Is that a question?" I said.

The kid shrugged.

"I don't follow."

"The way you said Thailand just now sounded like you

didn't really know where he was; either that or you're lying."

"Why would I lie?"

"I don't know," I said. "You tell me."

He didn't respond. Cade smiled, indicating his approval of my interrogation techniques.

"Why's your uncle in Thailand?" I said.

"I dunno."

"When will he be back?"

"I dunno."

"How long has he been there?" I said.

"I dunno."

"What do you know?" I said.

"To tell you the truth, I don't know anything."

"You're breathing pretty heavy for someone who doesn't know anything," I said. "Would you like a glass of water?"

He shook his head.

"I need to go bring the horses in. Can I go now?"

Cade and I both nodded.

After Henry went outside, Cade said, "Well, what do you think?"

CHAPTER THIRTY-THREE

"He's lying," I said.

"You got that impression too—what was your first clue?"

"The heavy breathing every time I asked him a question. You?"

"His eyes."

"Shifty," I said.

"Exactly. The question is, what are we going to do about it?"

"I want to show you something," I said.

We walked upstairs and I pointed to the photograph hanging in the middle of the photo-collage on the wall. It was the one of the family standing in front of a house in the middle of a forest of trees. "Do you know where this is?"

Cade rubbed his chin and looked it over. "Kinda looks like Alpine. Why are you so interested?"

"I don't know. Something about this picture shouts 'private retreat.' It's worth looking into. Is it far?"

"Fifty miles or so. But it's too dark to go tonight."

"That's fine," I said, taking the picture off the wall. "What are you doing tomorrow?"

Cade picked me up the following morning at daylight.

"They want me to report in," he said, "and brief the FBI on what I know about the case."

"What did you say?"

"I said I'd be in after lunch."

"How did that go over?"

He shrugged.

"I didn't stick around to find out," he said. "I called a real estate agent as well to see what I could find out about the Kents owning another place."

"And?"

"He hasn't got back to me yet, and I don't want to wait."

The next several minutes were spent in silence. I stared at the picture of the house amongst the trees hoping I'd be able to spot it when we reached our destination. Cade tapped his fingers on the steering wheel to the beat of what I assumed was a twangy country concert taking place inside of his head.

"Do you know why I came back here?" he said.

"To help your dad with the case, right?"

"Well, yes. But, there's another reason."

I didn't want to say it before he did, just in case I was wrong.

"My dad's sick," he said.

He glanced over at me, studying my face for a reaction, which I wish he hadn't done. I'd never been good at hiding anything—especially on my face.

"You know," he said, "don't you?"

I nodded. "Did your dad tell you?"

"My mom did," he said. "I think my dad's been tryin' to tell me, but he hasn't been able to. My mom thought I needed to know just in case somethin' happens before it's supposed to."

"Are you going to talk to your dad about it—tell him you know?"

Cade shook his head.

"I figure my dad will say somethin' in his own time. There's no reason it has to be right now. Not with everything else that's goin' on."

"How's your mother doing?"

"Better now that I'm here," he said. "She's a tough woman, but my dad means everything to her. I'm not sure how strong she'll be once he's gone."

"What about your daughter—does she know?"

"Not much. She can tell he's sick. She's asked me about it a couple times, but we've never really had a discussion. Guess I need to talk to her about it."

"I wish there was something that could be done for him."

"Yeah," Cade said, glancing out the window. "Me too."

"Are you glad you moved back? I mean—do you like it here?"

He extended one of his hands and said, "What's not to like? The air is clean, people are simple and uncomplicated. I've been to big cities. They're all crowded. Too many people. Too much traffic. Out here things feel like they move at a slower pace. I have time to enjoy life."

I laughed.

"You're so passionate; you've almost convinced me to move here."

"What about you? Do you like Park City?" he said.

"I do, but I wasn't raised there. I grew up in a small town in California."

He raised a brow. "So, why Park City?"

"My grandfather lived there. I wanted to be close to him while he was still alive. After I moved, I fell in love, and I've lived there ever since."

Cade looked out the window. "We're here. I can't guarantee we're going to find the place, but we can sure try."

We drove up one street and down another, trying to match the house up with the surroundings in the photograph. Thirty minutes in, our quest hadn't yielded any positive results, but we kept looking anyway. Alpine wasn't a very big town, but there was one thing it had a plenty of: trees. The rich, vibrant shades of green blanketed most of the valley. It was breathtaking.

"How many people live here—in Alpine?" I said.

"Less than a thousand, I'd imagine." Cade pulled over to the side of the road and pointed. "This is where the three rivers meet—the Snake River, Salt River, and Greys River. They all come together and run into Palisades Reservoir."

We sat there for a moment, taking it all in.

"I caught a good-sized mac here over the summer," Cade said.

"A what?"

"C'mon, you serious? A mackinaw."

"I still don't follow."

"It's a lake trout," he said. "Haven't you done any fishin' before?"

"Not really."

He smiled.

"Greys River has some of the best fishin' around," he said. "I'll have to take you sometime."

I didn't know what to say, so I didn't say anything. Cade pulled back onto the road, and we were on our way again.

"I don't mean to disappoint you, but we've driven around just about every street there is here."

"What about that one?" I said, pointing to a shiny piece of metal reflecting off the upper side of one of the mountains.

Cade leaned forward, squinting. "I don't see anything."

"It's right there," I said. But when I looked again, it was gone. "I saw something about halfway up that mountain. I swear. It's hidden by all those trees."

He tugged on the inside of his pocket, pulling out his phone. "Let me try that agent one more time." It went to voicemail. "I wasn't aware there were any roads up there, but let's head that way and see if we can find one. If not, we'd better head back."

We drove a couple miles before the road forked. The flash of light I'd seen had been to the right, so Cade turned. I kept looking, hoping to catch a glimpse of what I saw before, but I didn't. It was like the sun had shifted, and the light was no longer hitting it just right. We drove up a steep hill. It didn't seem propitious at first, but when we reached the top, there it was: the house. I glanced at it, and then down at the picture, verifying they were one and the same. They were.

The home was modest, no more than a couple thousand square feet, which was all on one level. No cars were parked out front, but a closed, oversized garage offered a bit of encouragement. We drove up the paved driveway, parked, and got out.

"All this because we matched a fingerprint," I said.

No one came to the door when we knocked. Cade jiggled the handle. It was unlocked. We went in.

I cupped my hand over my mouth and shouted, "Hello?"

Nothing.

"Is anyone here?" Cade said.

Still nothing.

The entryway opened to a living room that split off into two hallways. I took one side, Cade took the other. The first room I came to was a closet of some kind. It was filled with oversized metal cans of food storage, fishing poles, and neatly stacked plastic bins. Typed labels were on the front of each bin, revealing the contents of the container. Most were labeled with the names of different holidays, the majority of them being Christmas.

The holiday bins had a second row of plastic containers behind them. I assumed they'd reveal even more of the same kind of thing, but I decided to look just in case. I pulled one from the first row off the shelf. Behind it was a bin labeled: Grace. I took it down and opened it. Inside I found stacks of folded clothes, most of them in a size five. I put the lid back on and slid the next one off the shelf. The bin behind it was labeled: Makayla. Makayla's box contained clothes in a larger size, but there was something else.

At the bottom of the box was a broken picture frame. I instantly recognized one of the girls in the picture. But it wasn't one of the Kents' daughters; it was Savannah Tate.

Savannah appeared to be alive and well in the photograph standing next to who I assumed was Olivia Hathaway. The labels on the boxes told me their names had been changed, but that wasn't all. Both girls had dark, brown hair before they were taken, and now they were blondes. But it didn't matter what the Kents did to change the girls' appearances, there was no mistaking Savannah's angelic face. She looked just like she did in the photo her mother had been holding.

If the Kents had moved the girls to this hideaway in the woods, where were they?

I walked out of the storage room, planning to find Cade, but stopped when I noticed a closed door at the end of the hall. I was curious, so I walked to it, turning the knob when I got there. I slowly pushed the door open. The door creaked like the hinge plates needed to be oiled. I turned on the light, illuminating the master bedroom, and then gasped, throwing my hand over my nose to mask the indescribable odor. The scene before me was horrific. On the bed, Bradley and Regina Kent lay next to one another. Their eyes were closed. But they weren't sleeping; they were dead.

CHAPTER THIRTY-FOUR

I sprinted down the hall, darting around the room in search of Cade. My eyes were blurred, and I couldn't see much of anything out of them. I thought about yelling, but that would have required me to get actual words out, and I could hardly breathe, let alone form sentences.

In a matter of moments my elation over finding the photo of both missing girls had turned from hope to heartache. Someone had found the one place the Kents had chosen to hide the girls from everyone else. Were the girls dead too?

I paused, leaning over the kitchen counter to gain control over my staggered breathing, but resting did nothing to quell the anxiety growing inside me. A sound echoed from the opposite end of the house. I followed it to Cade, who was bent over looking inside bedroom drawers.

"Where are they?" I shouted when I entered the room.

"Who?"

"The girls! Their bodies! Have you found them yet?"

Cade gripped the sides of my arms, shaking me. "Sloane, look at me. What are you talking about—what's happened?"

I breathed in and out; slow and steady, closing my eyes for several seconds and then opening them back up again. I looked around. The room was decorated in a variety of colors, but one stood out far more than the rest: green. Olivia's room. The bed was disheveled, the comforter piled up at the bottom, and I couldn't see a flat sheet, only a fitted one. There was no sign of Olivia.

I dashed out of the room, throwing the door open to the second bedroom across the hall. I paid attention to nothing but another unmade bed in front of me. Again, empty.

Cade ran up behind me. "What's gotten into you? Sloane, talk to me!"

"Have you searched the rest of the house?" I said.

"What does that have to do with—"

"Have you searched it?!"

He nodded.

"Why?"

I was mumbling to myself now. "Good, then there is still hope…maybe they're alive. I need to check both of their rooms for clues. We need to find out who—"

"Sloane—what' going on?" Cade's voice was agitated.

"The girls—they've been taken."

"What girls?" he said.

"Olivia and Savannah."

"How do you know?"

"I found a picture of them in a storage room. They were together—they are together. The Kents took them and—the Kents!"

I grabbed Cade's shirt sleeve, pulling him down the hall

behind me. "I need to show you something."

I led him to the master bedroom, allowing him to enter before me. His reaction upon seeing the bodies was similar to mine, except I'd hesitated to get too close. Cade walked right up to them, staring down at their lifeless bodies. He leaned over, looking first at Regina, and then crossing to the other side of the bed to inspect Bradley.

"Well, I know how they died," he pointed to Bradley Kent's head. "A single gunshot wound to the head."

"It smells in here," I said. "I'd like to get a closer look at the bodies, but I don't know if I can take it."

Cade unbuttoned the top snap of his shirt, holding it up to his nose. He inhaled and exhaled out of it. "I might need to get some air myself," he said. "And then I need to call this in."

"Now?"

"Soon," he said. "Let's make sure we have everything we need first. What all have you touched?"

"Some bins in the storage room and a couple doorknobs."

"Wipe everything down," he said.

"Why?"

"With the feds in town, you shouldn't be here," he said. "They'll be all over you for this, and I don't want you involved."

"But, you said we would work—"

"All I'm saying is it would look better if I found this place on my own," he said. "I'm trying to protect you. We are in this together. Although, how I'll explain me ending up here, I have no idea. Time is everything right now, so we're out of here in fifteen minutes tops. I need to get the coroner here as soon as possible."

I searched the bathroom for a washcloth and found one in the third drawer. I also found a box of latex gloves under some bottles of blond hair dye. I gave the gloves to Cade so if he wanted a closer inspection of the bodies, he could touch them. Then I retraced my steps, making sure to wipe down only the surfaces I had touched. Now all investigators would find were the smudged oil spots that had been left by the pads of my fingers, nothing they'd be able to analyze.

Behind the living room was a large office. When I walked by, I noticed one of the drawers from the desk was lying on the floor, its contents spilled out all over the room. An office chair was also tipped on its side. I walked over, kneeling down to get a closer look. The drawer had come out of the center console in the desk. The front of the drawer had a busted lock. Someone had been looking for something. Papers were scattered around the drawer. I bent over, trying to see what they were without picking them up. There was a deed to some land, deeds to the Kents' vehicles, and a few other things of no consequence.

Had the thief gotten what he came for?

I started to stand back up and noticed a piece of fabric hanging off the office chair. At first I thought it had ripped, but upon closer inspection I could see that the upholstery covering the back of the chair velcroed at the bottom. A small piece at the end had folded over just enough to reveal a thin slit. And under the slit, a slight bulge. I pulled the Velcro up and a brown leather book fell out. It was smaller than an index card and thin. As I thumbed through it, most of the pages were empty except for a few handwritten ones at the beginning.

At the top of each page at the front of the book was a name. The name, which was always female, was followed by information like eye color, hair color, and age. There was no address or phone number, just a general description of each child. There was also a price which ranged from forty thousand dollars to one hundred thousand dollars. A few girls had question marks by their names. Six pages in, I came across Olivia's name. She didn't have a question mark. She had a star. A star to indicate she was the chosen one. Next to her name was a price: fifty thousand dollars. I flipped through a few more pages and found Savannah. She also had a star, but her price was one hundred thousand dollars. Younger children, it seemed, went for much more than their older counterparts. The thought of purchasing children at any price sickened me.

I took the book over to the printer and lifted the flap on the copy machine. One by one, I printed each page until they all had been printed. I removed the book, flipping through it one last time to make sure I hadn't missed anything before putting it back where I found it. On the last page of the book, in the corner on the bottom was a phone number. There was no name and no other information, just a phone number. I returned to the scanner and printed it out.

Cade was snapping photos of the Kents with his camera phone from all different angles when I walked back in.

"Find anything interesting?" I said.

"They both show signs of livor mortis."

"You mean rigor mortis?" I said.

He shook his head.

"At the livor mortis stage, the blood collects around the lowest part of the body. See the discoloration here?" He pointed at Bradley Kent's legs. "This is how I can tell."

There were areas of skin on Bradley's lower body that were reddish in color, like they had been burned, even though they hadn't. Other areas were white and completely drained of color.

"It looks like splotchy rosacea," I said.

"Splotchy, yes. Rosacea, no."

"What does that tell you?"

"Their bodies are stiff, but not as hard as some others I've seen," he said. "My best guess? They've been dead for less than three days, but I'd put their deaths at less than a day."

"From the looks of things, someone did it while they were sleeping," I said.

Cade nodded in agreement.

"There's also nothing to suggest their bodies were moved after they were shot. The killer either didn't care if they were found, or didn't have time to clean up the mess."

"Someone knows we are looking for Olivia and Savannah," I said. "And they know we're close."

CHAPTER THIRTY-FIVE

Cade and I were on our way back to the hotel so he could drop me off. The shock of what I'd just seen weighed on my mind. What the Kents had done was unforgivable, but I still felt a sense of sadness over the children they lost and the way their life had come to an end.

Several new theories crossed my mind. It was my opinion that Regina had sent the coloring pages to both parents over the guilt she felt about stealing another person's child. She probably didn't understand the impact of her actions. If she had, I was sure she would not have done it.

The kidnapper most likely had certain "rules" he expected the Kents to follow. One of those rules would have been having no contact with the former family. When Regina sent the coloring page to the Hathaways and the news of it leaked to the paper, it alerted the kidnapper that their agreement had been broken. Without knowing it, Regina had put a target on their heads.

I also wondered about the kidnapping itself—whether the Kents were in on it together when Olivia was taken, or if

Bradley, distraught with his grieving wife, had contacted the kidnapper the first time himself. But I suppose none of that mattered now.

As soon as Cade backed out of the Kents' driveway, he called the double homicide in, saying he'd received an anonymous call from someone who alleged they knew where the girls were. The chief was suspicious, asking several questions, but Cade stood his ground, and he was convincing enough for the chief to take him seriously.

After thinking it over, Cade decided it would be best if the feds arrived at the home thinking they were first on scene, having no idea we'd ever been there at all. Cade offered to drive up to the house, but the federal agent in charge got on the line, thanked him, and said, "We'll take it from here."

Of course they would. We intended to do the same.

Cade and I did our best to leave everything the way we found it, the bodies included. Not much time had passed since we'd arrived there, which I felt good about. Neither of us wanted to do anything to hurt the investigation. Within the hour, agents would be picking apart the place, piece by piece. I was anxious to know whether they'd discover what I had.

"The fact the girls weren't there is a good sign," I said. "Maybe they're still alive."

"Let's hope so," Cade replied.

"I think whoever took Olivia and Savannah found out about the page that was mailed to Olivia's parents and probably saw it as some kind of violation of their agreement."

Cade shook his head.

"I know you believe the Kents paid someone to take Olivia

and Savannah, but we still don't know for sure."

"I think we do." I opened my bag and pulled out the pages I copied. "I found a book hidden inside the fabric of a chair in Bradley Kent's office. It contains the names of several girls along with their ages and prices."

"And what are those?" he said pointing to the papers in my hand.

"Copies. I put the book back where I found it when I was done."

"Names and basic information—that all?"

I shook my head.

"There's one more thing—a phone number. I found it on the last page. It's written in pencil, and on the light side, but I can still make the numbers out."

Cade swerved off the road, jerking the truck to a stop.

"What are you doing?" I said.

He held his hand out. "Let's try it, see what happens."

"The number?"

"Why not? Who knows how long those girls have before somethin' happens to them—that's if they're even still alive."

I handed him the copied page. He glanced at it and then dialed. Once it started ringing, he put the call on speaker. The phone rang four times, then it clicked, and the line was quiet. A few seconds later, the call disconnected.

"It sounded like someone answered the call and hung it up," I said.

"Then let's try it again, so he'll know we're serious."

This time it rang twice, and the same thing happened. Cade dialed a third time. It rang once and the line was silent, but the phone stayed connected.

"Hello" Cade said. "Is anyone there?"

"Who's this?"

The voice on the other end was a man's. It was raspy, like a life-long chain smoker who was now paying the price.

"I'm calling to inquire about your services," Cade said.

"You're lying."

"I'm not. I have a proposition for you."

"Cut the shit—who are you and how'd you get my number?"

"Who are you?" Cade said.

There was no response.

"I'm interested in two little girls," Cade said. "Blond hair, ages four and eight. Can you accommodate me?"

The man remained quiet.

"Just tell me when, and where, and how much," Cade said.

I wanted to grab the phone and scream into it, let the guy on the other end know how I felt about how he made his living. Remaining quiet required an amount of patience I lacked, but I didn't have a choice—I couldn't compromise the children.

"You still there?" Cade said. "Are you considering my offer?"

The phone disconnected, and the next several times Cade called back, it just kept on ringing.

"He's shut his phone off," I said. "Probably tossing it right now."

"Maybe."

202   Cheryl Bradshaw

Cade made a call to the department, asking someone to run the number for him. He was put on hold, and a few minutes later, the person returned to the line. They said something, and he asked them to look into it. Then he ended the call."

"Anything?" I said.

"I got a name."

"What is it?"

"Jack Sparrow."

"As in Captain Jack Sparrow?" I said.

"I'm guessin' so. And I'll bet there's no way to link it back to an actual person."

I looked at him. "Try the number one more time."

He called one last time. "Now I'm getting an out-of-service message."

"Thought so," I said.

CHAPTER THIRTY-SIX

If the man on the other end of the line did have Olivia and Savannah, and they were alive, I wasn't sure they'd stay that way for long. He was in the business of pickup and delivery, not parenting. He'd already proven he had no problem killing old ladies and adults, and he may have spared the children for now, but for how long?

Several hours had passed without me hearing from Cade. I thought about trying his number, but I wasn't sure what happened after he'd dropped me off and went to the station. With the feds in town, I had no way of knowing how everything would play out.

I remembered the business card Cade's father had given me and decided I'd try him instead. I took it out of my wallet and made the call, but the phone was answered by a woman.

"I'm sorry," I said. "I believe I have the wrong number."

"Who are you trying to reach?"

Her voice was low and quiet, making it difficult for me to understand what she was saying.

"Detective McCoy," I said.

"This is his phone. Who's calling?"

"Sloane Monroe."

"You're my son's friend," she said, "aren't you?"

"I am."

"It seems I'm always out running errands when you stop by."

"I was looking for Cade. I thought your husband might know if he is still at the station or not."

"He's here," she said. "Would you like to speak with him?"

"Are you all at home?"

There was a pause and then she said, "No, dear. We're at the hospital."

Over the next several minutes I had an inner debate with myself, trying to decide whether it would be appropriate for me to show up at the hospital offering my support. I'd gotten to know Cade and his father to a degree, but it was a small one, and I wasn't family. Maybe he hadn't contacted me because, right now, he didn't want me around.

Still, we'd become friends over the past several days, and I never did very well sitting idly by while a friend was in need. I picked my jacket off the edge of the sofa and walked out the door.

The first person I saw when I entered the hospital was Shelby, Cade's daughter. She took one look at me and her face turned fifty shades of pissed-off teenager. I thought about avoiding her, but to my surprise, she got out of the chair and walked over to me.

"I'm not trying to cause any problems by being here," I said.

Shelby crossed her arms in front of her. "Yeah, whatever." She half-pointed to a side room. "My dad's in there."

"Are you okay?"

She looked at me like I was crazy.

"Why? Are you going to do something for me if I'm not?"

She was hurting. Now was the time to keep my mouth shut. I smiled and walked away.

Cade was inside the hospital room with his mother. They were holding hands as she dabbed her nose and eyes with a tissue. At that point, I didn't even know if Detective McCoy was still alive. But I didn't feel right about being there. I backed out, hoping no one would notice I was ever there.

I passed by Shelby on my way out and waved, trying to smile. She held the back of her hand out like she was going to flip me off, but instead made a gesture like she just wanted me to go away—fast. I walked out the door feeling like an idiot for meddling in someone else's private business. The inner dialogue of self-criticism continued while I walked until I realized someone had been calling my name.

I pivoted on my heeled shoe. Cade was standing in front of me, out of breath. He didn't say anything. He just wrapped his arms around me, pulling me tight. I wasn't sure how long we stood there, neither of us speaking, just me supporting him with a friendly embrace. Maybe I was needed after all.

When Cade released me, I resisted the temptation of asking the question, and instead waited for him to speak.

"I'm glad you're here," he said. "I was going to call you, but—"

"You don't need to concern yourself with me right now."

"My dad, he's not making any sense. One minute he's talking to me about things that happened when he was a child, and he has a perfect recollection of past events. The next minute, he looks at me like he doesn't know who I am. He called me Joey. I don't even know a Joey. None of us does. I knew it was going to get bad and, they'd prepped us for it, but I never expected this."

He was still alive.

I knew it would be hard for me to look Cade in the eye; it always was in a situation like this, but I had to. His eyes were pale and wet, but I knew he wouldn't cry. He was strong—too strong to let his emotions show right now. They would come later, when the dam finally broke, allowing his pent-up feelings to come flowing out.

"How long has it been since your father has eaten anything?" I said. "He looked so thin when I stopped by last."

"Two—three days. I'm not sure. He lost his appetite. My mom's tried everything; he's not interested."

"Maybe eating makes him feel sick," I said.

Cade's mother stepped into the parking lot and looked at him. "He's asking for you," she said.

"I'd better go," I said, "but you can call me anytime you need to. I mean it."

Cade's mom shook her head. "Please don't go. He wants to speak to you both—together."

I didn't think it was for the best, but there was no way I

could turn her down, or him. We walked together to his room, my apprehension growing with every step. I'd never cared much for hospitals, but then, who did?

Detective McCoy mustered a smile when we walked in. He looked pleased to see both of us. I hoped the conversation we were about to have was one of his more coherent ones.

"Come in, come in," he said, motioning both of us over to the bed.

We did what he asked, standing next to the bed, and awaiting his next statement.

"Chief Rollins tells me they found the people who took Savannah," he said, his voice surprisingly strong.

"And Olivia, the other missing girl from Sublette County. Neither one of the children were there when the feds searched the house, but they found photographic evidence that both girls had been living there, among other things."

Cade and I looked at each other. I tried to act surprised.

"The chief said they lifted a lot of usable prints which he's running now."

"I thought the feds didn't want us involved?" Cade said.

"We're not. But they don't mind sharing a few bread crumbs with Rollins." Detective McCoy looked at me. "Cade shared some other things with me earlier today."

Cade and I exchanged looks.

Detective McCoy took my hand in his, grabbing Cade's with the other. He put them together, mine on the bottom, Cade's on top. For a moment it didn't feel like I was standing in front of a hospital bed. It felt like I was in a church awaiting the marriage ceremony to begin.

"What's this about, Dad?" Cade said.

"It's about the two of you seein' this through," Detective McCoy said. "I'm too weak to continue on, not that the feds would have let me anyway. But, if it wasn't for my illness, I would have found a way. It's up to the two of you now. Don't let that man kill those girls. Once you figure out who he is, you find them."

"We'll do everything we can," I said.

Detective McCoy looked at me and then at Cade. "Promise me. Both of you. No matter what happens to me, your first priority is Savannah and Olivia."

Cade squeezed my hand, looked at his father, and said, "We promise."

CHAPTER THIRTY-SEVEN

Although Detective McCoy wanted us to stay focused on the girls, I knew Cade wasn't up to it, no matter what he said to the contrary. We finished talking to Detective McCoy, and Cade walked me to my car. He said he'd been sent over a list of names of inmates who had been released within the past five years, all with the same tattoo. He even had photos. Excellent. I convinced him to give me the list. He was reluctant, but he wasn't ready to leave his father.

I sat at the small table in my hotel room looking over the list of names in front of me. It was long. I had no idea the clock tattoo was so popular, but with two million inmates in prison across the United States, it was no wonder there were so many.

I'd taken a class once on prison methods and had learned a few things about prison tattoos. For one, it was illegal, but that didn't stop inmates from doing it anyway. Men who entered prison having prior tattoos were much more likely to get another one while incarcerated than their non-tattooed counterparts, even though there were risks involved. Nonsterile methods were used, such as using paper clips as applicators and soot mixed with shampoo for the ink. This often caused deadly diseases such as hepatitis and HIV/AIDS.

I looked over my stacked sheets of hay, feeling less than confident that I'd be able to find the needle among them. People in the business of stealing children weren't easily traced due to the fact they rarely owned anything. They lived like transients, driving from place to place, staying in hotel rooms under assumed names, paying cash for whatever they needed. And only one thing mattered to a person like that: his next payday.

I stood up, leaving the list of names on the table. I wanted to grab the papers and hurl them across the room. I hated to admit it, but I actually hoped the feds would find something Cade and I had missed when they searched the house—anything to bring Olivia and Savannah home.

Think, Sloane, think.

I returned to the table, remembering I had a connection to the kidnapper. Now I just needed to use it.

"Jenny, I need a favor," I said.

She yawned into the phone. "What, umm, time is it?"

"It's late. Please, I don't have much time."

"Sure, yeah. What do you need?"

"I need you to talk to Todd."

"What—why? I haven't spoken to him in—"

"I know," I said, "but this is important."

"What is it?"

"I am sending several photos to your phone. I need you

to show them to Todd. Ask him if he recognizes any of the men from the night Olivia was abducted."

"Why don't you just call him yourself?" she said. "I have his number."

"After what I put him through, I'm not sure he'll agree to speak to me, but I'm willing to bet he'll talk to you."

"Got it. I'm on my way."

I paced the floor for the next hour, going over all the photos I'd sent Jenny, cross-checking them with the photos I hadn't sent. I wanted to be sure I hadn't missed any possibilities. Narrowing the list by age and height alone left a couple dozen possibilities. I then cut it down even more by the crimes they'd committed to put them in prison in the first place. I just hoped one of them was our man.

I was about to try Jenny's phone when my own rang.

"Jenny?" I said.

"It's Todd."

"I didn't think you'd be interested in talking to me or I would have called you myself."

"I'm not."

"Did you look at the pictures I sent?" I said.

"Yep."

"Did you recognize anyone?"

"Yep."

A wave of excitement rushed through me. I just hoped he was right.

"Are you absolutely certain?"

"Yep."

"How do you know?"

"The guy was wearing glasses, so I covered the top half of their faces. His chin—there was something about it. I tried explaining it to the sketch artist, and I couldn't get it right."

"But you saw it in one of the photos?" I said.

"The third one—it's him."

CHAPTER THIRTY-EIGHT

Cade came by the next morning.

"I was going to call you a few hours ago," I said. "But I figured you were asleep, so I decided to wait."

"You were awake—why?"

"I'll explain in a minute. How's your dad?"

"They won't release him yet, but the nurse said he's awake and talking to everyone. I hope it's a good sign."

"Me too," I said.

"What did you make of the names I gave you?"

I grabbed a paper from the table and handed it to him.

He scanned it, muttering the contents of the rap sheet to himself. When he finished, he said, "Eddie Fletcher. How do you know this is the guy?"

I told him about my conversation with Todd the previous night.

"Anything new on your end?" I said.

"Chief Rollins called me this morning. The coroner looked over both bodies. He concluded the time of death was between ten and midnight the night before we showed up.

The coroner said the same thing I did—the Kents were sleeping at the time of death. So far no prints have been found that can't be accounted for."

I was relieved for us, but not for the killer.

Cade mentioned a few more details from the ME's report, but nothing I considered alarming.

"The question is: where do we go from—"

I was interrupted by the sound of Cade's phone. He grabbed it out of his pocket so fast, he almost dropped it. I imagined he was waiting for an update on his dad, but it wasn't the hospital or his mother on the other end of the line. It was the sound of someone saying Cade's name. He flipped over a piece of paper on the desk, and wrote one word on it: EDDIE.

I assumed Cade recognized his voice from their previous conversation. I moved closer.

"Cade McCoy?" Eddie said, again.

"Who's this?"

"Find a pen and paper. You have five seconds."

Cade sat down at the desk and flipped the phone on its side so I could hear the conversation.

"Do you have it yet?" Eddie said.

"Yes."

"Good. Don't talk, just listen."

Neither of us moved.

"Are you listening?" Eddie said.

"You said no talking," Cade said.

"At seven o'clock tonight, you will bring two hundred and fifty thousand dollars in cash to a shack at the end of

Swanee Bridge Road."

"How do you expect me to come up with the money in such a short—"

"Not my problem," Eddie said. "And you're not talking, remember?"

Cade stayed quiet.

"You'll get to the location using my directions. Head North on Tucker Road heading out of town. Drive twelve miles. When you get to Falcon Drive, turn right. The next road you come to will be Swanee Bridge. The place you are looking for is at the end of the road. It's old and run down. You won't have trouble finding it."

Cade and I exchanged glances, but neither of us dared say anything. Eddie continued.

"Listen to this next part carefully. You will not involve the media, the police, the FBI, or anyone else. This is between us. If I see anyone come in with you, the girls die. If you don't bring the money, the girls die."

Eddie paused, then continued.

"The money will not have any consecutive numbers. The money bag will not contain an explosive dye. There will be no new bills, no marked bills, and no tracking devices of any kind, either in the money bag or in your vehicle. Do you understand?"

Cade looked at me like he wasn't sure whether to speak or not.

"Yes or no?" Eddie said.

"Yes—now can I ask you a question?"

"Depends on what it is."

"Where will the children be?" Cade said.

"When you get to the shack, go up the steps to the porch and stick the money through the window. It will be open. Then walk back to your car. Wait ten minutes and then enter the house. The girls will be waiting inside. Do we have a deal?"

"Yes."

"I'll be watching your every move. Their life is in your hands, Mr. McCoy."

"I want proof," Cade said.

"What's that?"

"I'm not bringin' the money unless I know the girls are still alive. Put one of them on the phone."

"That's not going to happen."

"Then forget it."

Cade hung up.

"What are you doing?!" I yelled, reaching for the phone.

"Give it a minute—he'll call back. He wants the money, trust me."

I wasn't so sure. We waited two minutes, and then five. No phone call. I drank an entire glass of water, rinsed dishes, and tried to keep my mouth shut. It wasn't easy. I was losing my mind, and in another minute, I'd be losing it on him.

And then the phone rang.

"Told you," Cade said, reaching for his phone.

He answered it and pressed the speaker button.

"Hello?"

"Hello?"

There it was. A beautiful, young female voice.

"Who's this?" Cade said.

"Makayla. I mean Olivia."

"Are you okay?" Cade said.

"I don't know, I guess so. Who are you?"

"Someone who has been tryin' to find you and Savannah," Cade said. "Is she with you now?"

"Yes."

There was a sound like the phone was exchanging hands. "All right, you talked to her. We have a deal. Seven o'clock. Don't be late."

The phone clicked.

"I can't believe this is happening," I said.

But Cade didn't hear me. He sat down, drumming his fingers on the table in front of him.

"What's going on?" I said.

"I'm just tryin' to decide the best way to work this out."

"What do you mean?"

"I want to make sure I handle this right. Two hundred and fifty thousand is a lot of cash to come up with in a short amount of time."

"We will think of something," I said.

He still wasn't listening.

"I just hope they'll go for it without hearing the conversation."

"Who?" I said.

"The FBI."

"This Fletcher guy said not to involve them," I said. "It's too big of a risk, Cade. You can't."

"He doesn't care if I use them to get the money."

I shook my head.

"If he didn't care, he wouldn't have told you to leave them out of it," I said.

"He just wants to make sure I drive out there alone, and I will."

"They'll never let you," I said. "There's no way they'll hand over the money and allow you to make the rules. That's not how they do things."

Cade shrugged.

"Doesn't matter…they'll have to. It's my way or it's no way at all."

CHAPTER THIRTY-NINE

Cade left without me convinced that letting the feds in on the situation was the best solution. He was sure they would understand once he explained everything. Cade's version of "everything" would be telling them that the kidnapper knew who he was because he'd been working the case for the past several weeks...and that he was the only one who could do the drop off because the guy knew what he looked like. Cade had a way with words, but I wasn't convinced it would work this time.

Cade expected me to stay put. He thought it was safer for the girls if I didn't get involved, but taking orders had never been my strong suit. The kidnapper expected Cade at a certain time. He knew it would take him several hours to get his hands on the kind of cash he requested. He didn't seem to know about me or my involvement in the case, and I wanted it to stay that way.

As soon as Cade left, I searched the Internet for Swanee Bridge Road. The map I found was a little less detailed than I'd hoped for, but it pointed me in a general direction. I scribbled down the directions on a piece of paper, grabbed my keys and my gun, and left.   I drove until I reached a point where my cell reception started fading and gave Cade a quick call to check in.

"What a nightmare," he said when he answered the phone.

"They aren't letting you go alone, are they?" I said.

"Not a chance. They even told me I couldn't go. Can you believe it? They were going to send one of their guys in my place and leave me out of it all together."

"What did you say?" I said.

"I told them the kidnapper was calling me at seven o'clock and that if someone else answered, he'd know it wasn't me. I also told them he knew what I looked like."

"Nice job, liar," I said. "Did they buy it?"

"I think so. They're off in another room discussin' it now. Where are you?"

"I stopped at the store for a couple things, grabbed a bite to eat."

"If they let me go, and I think they will, I probably won't be able to call you again until it's all over," he said. "They've been following me around ever since I got here."

Perfect.

"I'll be waiting for your call," I said. "Good luck."

Thankfully Cade was too preoccupied with the feds and all their minions to consider it odd that I'd so easily backed off, allowing him to see it through to the end on his own. I passed Falcon, opting for an alternative side road to turn on instead of the street the kidnapper suggested. According to the map the next road circled back at some point, leading me to the same place. I had to assume Eddie might already be there waiting. An alternate route was my best chance to go unnoticed.

The area around me looked like some kind of national forest. Several roads had no signage of any kind. Luckily, Falcon was marked with a wooden stake, its letters painted yellow. I passed it and took the next left, picking a cluster of trees and hiding my car behind them. I'd walk the rest of the way.

It took over an hour, but I finally reached the end of Swanee Bridge Road. The shack looked more like a one-hundred-year-old pile of abandoned wood. As for the window the kidnapper said he'd leave open—it was open all right—it was broken, shattered completely.

I took my time inspecting every angle of the area around me before taking a step closer. I listened for sounds coming from the house, for any sign of the girls or their abductor, but it was silent. The only noise I heard was coming from the birds in the trees around me. No one was there. Not yet.

I pushed open a wood door that had a hole where a handle had once been and looked around. There was nothing to the place at all. It was a simple, square room with no bedrooms and no other doors. It looked like there had been a kitchen at one time, but all of the cabinets had been ripped out. Some of the wood planks lining the floor were gone, maybe because of old age. I wasn't sure. They appeared to have rotted and fallen through to the ground below.

In the corner of the room was a wooden box, the only

accessory left in the place. I assumed it had been used for firewood at one time. I pulled the lid open and looked inside. There was still wood in it, but not a lot. I shifted a few pieces of wood around thinking insects would come crawling out of every orifice, but none did.

The box didn't appear to be the most comfortable place a person could hide, and it wasn't as sanitary as I would have liked, but I didn't have much choice. I considered taking the wood out, but didn't want to leave any clues that the box had been recently opened. Instead I turned the wood over splinter-side down, rearranging it into a smooth pile all the way across. Then I climbed inside.

I sat in a squatted position for two leg-numbing hours before I heard movement outside. The front door to the shack opened and footsteps walked inside. It was quiet for a moment and then a man yelled, "It's empty."

Another person said, "Let's get in position before the sonofabitch gets here."

Orders were called out, positions were assigned, and the door closed. There was a lot of rustling around while everyone got into place. Because the shack only consisted of one room, no one remained inside. I didn't know if they were cops or SWAT or what. Jackson didn't strike me like the kind of place that had a SWAT team on hand, and to call one in from Salt Lake would have taken time, even if they flew there. Wherever the kidnapper was, I hoped the presence of the FBI had gone undetected.

A vehicle drove down the path and parked in front of the house some time later. A car door shut. According to the time of my watch, Cade wouldn't arrive for another ten minutes. The front door opened again. Someone walked in, closing the door behind him. He sounded out of breath, or nervous, or both. But he was alone. If it was the kidnapper, where were the children?

The man paced back and forth for several minutes, stopping only when a second car came to a halt. Cade. The car door opened and closed. I heard footsteps ascend the stairs and then the sound of something hitting the floor inside the house.

"I've set the money inside the window," Cade said. "Now I'm walkin' back to my car."

"No you ain't," Eddie said.

Someone, who I assumed was Cade, was heaved across the room. "You lied to me," Eddie said.

"I could say the same to you," Cade said. "The girls aren't here."

"The address to where they're located is on this piece of paper," Eddie said.

I heard the sound of paper being rubbed together in someone's hand.

"But you're not getting it," Eddie said. "We had a deal. You broke it."

"I don't know what you're talkin' about," Cade said. "I brought your money—it's right there."

"But that's not all you brought, is it? I said no cops!"

Come on, Cade. Keep it together.

"I don't see anyone."

"Do you think I'm stupid or somethin'? I know

camouflage when I see it."

Cade sighed.

"It was the only way I could get you the money," he admitted. "I told them not to come, and they said they understood. I can still get you out of here as long as you tell me where the girls are."

Eddie laughed. It was a low, husky, sarcastic kind of laugh.

"Out of here and back in prison," he said. "Sorry, don't think so."

"You'll be alive."

"I'd be dead before I got out again. I'm not going back."

"Then you'll die."

"Where's your gun?" Eddie said.

Cade didn't answer.

"I said where's your gun, tough guy? Hand it over. Now."

I wasn't sure that now registered in Cade's vocabulary. There was some movement and then the sound of something hard sliding across the floor. A gun?

"You make a move like that again, you're a dead man," Eddie said. "Don't move."

Someone walked to the window—my guess was Eddie.

"I know you're out there," Eddie shouted. "You hear me, assholes! It's time I made a new deal. Get out of here, now! Or you'll never see those brats again. You hear me?!"

During Eddie's angry tirade I pushed the lid on the box open a tiny bit. My gun was drawn and ready just in case my timing was off. Thankfully, the man had his back to me. He was staring out the window, waiting for a reply. I peeked at Cade. He was sitting on the floor in a corner on the other side of the room staring right at me. The look on his face was hard to describe—it was a mixture of shock and anger. I waved. And then I realized how dumb it must have looked. He had a gun pointed at him, and I was waving and smiling like a blonde in a beauty pageant.

A minute went by. Then two. No one outside made any attempt to communicate. I assumed they were holding their positions, probably trying to figure out what to do. They hadn't fired which meant they either didn't have a clear shot or were waiting for visual confirmation of the girls.

Eddie walked back across the room, and for the first time, I had a decent view of him. He was big. The Paul Bunyan kind of big. No wonder Cade didn't have the upper hand.

"I guess they don't care about you," Eddie said, "so the two of us are going to take a little walk. We can get out the back by going under the house."

"But you're surrounded," Cade said.

The man laughed. "Not the way we're going. Now let's go."

Cade stood up, looking Eddie in the eye. "No."

"Then you're a dead man. We go out together, or you die."

Cade swung at the man, giving it everything he had. It was impressive, and for a moment I thought the man was shaken enough for Cade to knock the shotgun loose, until I heard the pump action of the gun loading the shell.

I didn't think. I didn't hesitate. I launched out of the box and fired, twice. The first bullet clipped Eddie's shoulder, stunning him, and the second hit him in the chest. Eddie didn't have time to react before his massive body collapsed to the ground. Cade knelt in front of him. I lowered my weapon. My hands were experiencing some kind of spasm. I holstered my gun and rubbed my hands together. It didn't help. And I knew why. I was fairly certain Eddie was dead or dying, and I'd never killed anyone before. I'd always wondered what it would be like and how I would feel after I'd done it. Maybe that's why I was shaking. I wasn't prepared for my own reaction. I thought I'd feel something more: remorse, regret, sorrow. But I didn't feel any of those things. I felt nothing.

The outside of the shack was abuzz. Men were talking, heading for the door. I dove for the piece of paper that moments earlier had slipped from Eddie's hand. Men ran through the doorway. Guns were aimed in my direction. After all, who was I and what was I doing here? Before the paper was ripped from my hands, I opened it, desperate to see what it said. But what I saw was my worst fear. The page was blank.

CHAPTER FORTY

I sat at the station waiting for Cade. It was morning, and it had been a long night. After the chief explained who I was and how I ended up there, I'd received an escort, in the back seat of a police SUV of all places. It was my first taste of what it felt like to be a common criminal, and hopefully my last. I was taken to an interrogation room and detained for several hours for questioning. The feds hadn't found my presence amusing, not even a little bit, and they still didn't know the half of it. In the end, I'd saved Cade's life, but they didn't care. They never did.

I was ordered to stay away from the case "or else." If they only knew how involved in it I really was, I wondered what they would have said then. I was told I couldn't leave town, not yet. They seemed to think they might not be done with me. But I was done with them.

Eddie Fletcher wasn't dead. He was in critical but stable condition. When I fired my gun, I'd tried to wound him enough to give Cade the upper hand, but to keep him alive just in case the paper turned out to be exactly what it was:

useless. The fact he was still alive gave us all something to hope for—not that it stopped me from running the moment I shot him over and over in my mind. If only my bullet could have wounded him instead of almost killing him. If only he could have told us where to find the children. If only the paper hadn't been blank.

If only.

I was released, pending possible contact if they needed anything else. Cade and I stopped by the hospital to see his father who was again referring to him as "Joey." I left the room almost as soon as we entered. Father and son needed time together. I wasn't sure how much more they'd have left.

Eddie's room was under twenty-four-hour surveillance, and with the feds involved, I wouldn't be able to get to him. Not that I hadn't considered trying. I went to the lobby, and waited until the nurse forced Cade from the room. "Detective McCoy needs his rest," she'd said. He'd persisted, saying his dad didn't want him to go. But no amount of pleading was enough to appease her. It was a speech she'd probably heard a hundred times before, one she was immune to.

Cade glanced around the waiting room, trying to spot me in a sea of unhappy people. His eyes looked different from the first time we'd met. They no longer had the same spark. They were a pale grey now, not the lustrous blue I'd remembered.

"Do you think he'll talk?" Cade said.

"Eddie?"

Cade nodded. I shook my head.

"He doesn't have a reason to. Even if they try and make him a deal, it won't be the kind he'll take. At this point, I don't think he cares. He's critical. He'd rather die than face more prison time. He doesn't give a damn about the children. I could probably walk in his room and choke what little life he has left out of him—he still won't tell me where they are."

It was a sad reality, and I didn't want to face it. I wanted to believe I could still find Olivia and Savannah. We knew who he was, and the feds were tearing apart every inch of his life for even the smallest clue, but would it lead them to the girls? I wasn't optimistic.

Cade pulled off the road next to where my car was parked, and I got out. Both of us were too deflated to say much of anything. I promised to call once I'd returned to the hotel. He nodded and drove away. I was just about to open the door to my car when something moved inside. Great, I thought. Even with the windows up, at least one animal had managed to find a way inside somehow. I stepped back, considering the various possibilities, but anything could have been nesting inside.

I approached the driver's-side window, cupping my hands over the glass. I looked in, but I couldn't see much. My window tint was too dark. I scanned the ground, looking for a fallen tree branch. I found one, picked it up, and made a plan. I'd yank the door handle open and sprint away, hoping whatever was inside would scamper out, hop out, or fly out. I didn't care, as long as it was out.

I pulled the door handle back and ran to the other side, using the tree branch like I was a baseball player up to bat. I watched. I waited. Nothing came out. Maybe whatever it was had been under the car, not in it. I crouched down, holding the stick out in front of me. I waved it around. Still nothing. With both eyes partially open, I leaned over, looked under the car, and was relieved when all I found were pine needles and forest debris.

I approached the driver's-side door again, stick in hand. Holding the stick out in front of me, I looked in. The driver's seat was empty. The passenger seat was empty. The back seat was full.

Two girls were lying down, clutching each other, shivering and cold. They stared at me, unsure of who I was or what I was doing there. Their arms were scraped up like they'd been walking through the trees at night in the dark. I suspected they had. The older child's cuts were dry. The younger had several scrapes on both arms, and even one on her leg, which was bleeding. It looked like the older girl had ripped a piece of clothing, tying it around the little one's ankle as best she could. I had expected to find them in pajamas since they had been whisked away at night, but one was wearing jeans, the other a summery dress. No wonder she was cold.

I threw my hands over my mouth and welcomed the tears that followed. Not their tears, mine. I'd found them—or they'd found me—at last.

Eddie Fletcher had let them go. Why? Because he was planning on killing Cade as soon as he had his money. Cade knew too much. Eddie knew he couldn't let him live, but something inside his sick, twisted mind allowed just enough mercy to spare the children. He probably thought he'd left them to die in these woods, but at least he didn't have the heart to do it himself.

The younger girl clutched the older girl's hand, squeezing it tight.

"It's okay. You are safe now," I said. "Don't be scared."

They looked at each other, saying nothing.

"My name is Sloane, and you must be Olivia," I said pointing to the older one.

She nodded.

I looked at the younger one. "And you're Savannah."

"How do you know our names?" Olivia said.

"I've been looking for you. Everyone has. Are you ready to go home?"

Olivia jerked back, shaking her head. "I'm not going back there."

"I'm sorry if I scared you. I didn't mean to. I'm taking you back to your real homes now."

I spent the next several minutes reassuring them, saying little about the search to find them and making sure to touch on only the details they needed to know. They'd suffered enough heartache—I'd leave the other details for their parents—let them decide.

I went to the trunk. When I returned to the front seat of the car, I handed something to Savannah.

"Mr. Fluffy!" she cried.

"Your friend Sierra gave this to me," I said. "She said it would keep you safe."

I promised again to take them home, to their real homes. They sat in the back seat side by side, holding hands. In the rear view mirror I caught a glimpse of Savannah, squeezing

Mr. Fluffy and smiling.

I made it out to the main road and called Cade.

"Is everything okay?" he said. "I didn't think I'd hear from you this soon."

"I found them, Cade!" I said. "Well, actually, they found me. I have Olivia and Savannah. They're safe!"

CHAPTER FORTY-ONE

I didn't know what it felt like to be the president of the United States, but when I arrived at the police station, I imagined it must have been similar to what I was feeling. Cops, feds, and office staffers stood outside, waiting, a look of disbelief on their faces. Noah Tate sprinted toward the car before it lulled to a stop, pulling the back door open. He gripped his little girl with both arms, pulling her toward him. Olivia's mother waited, cautious, a tissue clutched in her hand. I imagined the difference in her daughter from age six to age eight was staggering. But they were home, and they were safe. Nothing else mattered.

Olivia exited the car slowly, unsure at first. Mother and child didn't run to each other, they walked—as if in slow motion. Tears dripped down Kris's cheeks every step of the way. When she finally reached her daughter, she kneeled and held her for several minutes, neither wanting to let go.

Kris whispered something in Olivia's ear, and Olivia nodded. Then Kris walked over to me.

"I don't know how to thank you, Ms. Monroe," she said.

"I never believed I'd see my daughter again."

It wasn't something I felt I could take credit for, so I used the moment to shed light on something else.

"You can thank me by putting Olivia first," I said, "from here on out. Don't allow anyone to come between the two of you."

She nodded, understanding my meaning.

After the initial commotion died down and I made the rounds, Cade waved me over. We went outside. In the last hour, Eddie had passed away. No one seemed to care. Not anymore.

"So, I guess they've got a solid lead on the company Eddie Fletcher worked for," he said. "The company runs some kind of child trafficking operation—everything from babies to teenagers."

"I hope it gets shut down."

"Yeah, me too. You headed home today then?"

"I'm not sure yet. I guess so."

"We make a good team, you know?"

I winked.

"Are you offering me a job?"

He shrugged.

"I'm sure the chief is dying to hire a feisty woman without any legitimate law enforcement experience."

Cade put his arm around me. "You know what I mean."

"I feel the same way. I've never liked working with a partner before, but it's different with you."

He squeezed my shoulder and then let me go. "If you're ever *not* dating someone, you know where to find me."

I leaned in, kissing him on the cheek. "Maybe I will."

CHAPTER FORTY-TWO

I was an hour into my drive home when Cade called.

"Miss me already?" I said.

"My dad. He's—"

No! He couldn't be. Not yet.

I didn't want to finish the sentence, say the word "dead"—it seemed such a callous and inappropriate thing to say to someone who'd just lost a parent.

"Has he passed away?" I said.

"About an hour ago," Cade said. "I wasn't even there, Sloane. I didn't get to say goodbye."

My body stiffened, my hands unable to grip the wheel any longer. I pulled the car over. Cars whizzed past at high speed, but life had just slowed to a stop for me.

"I'm sorry, Cade. Are you okay?"

For the next several minutes, I offered a comforting ear, listening to Cade reminisce about some of the best memories he'd shared with his father. He mentioned everything from fly fishing to the time his dad taught him how to ride a bike. It was his way of dealing with the loss. At the end of the conversation, he didn't ask me to come back. He just said he didn't know who else to call, and he thanked me for listening.

The car idled. I squirmed in my seat, taking my seatbelt off and then putting it back on again. I didn't even know why I sat there. It wasn't my father who'd died, but what a difference our short time together had made. Cade had surprised me; he wasn't like other guys. It usually took me months, sometimes even years to form a lasting friendship with someone—man or woman. But he'd become just that— my friend. And I didn't have too many close ones.

A text message popped up on my phone. It was Lucio: Boss needs you to come home right away.

I replied: Why?

Lucio said: Talk about it when you get here. Giovanni asks how long you'll be.

Being under someone's thumb had never worked for me, even when it came to Giovanni. In the time we'd known one another, he'd always allowed me to lead my own life. But lately something had changed. It wasn't a control issue; it was something more, like he was watching out for me as if he *had* to. Maybe his sensitivity was heightened because of what happened to Daniela. I wasn't sure.

I had a decision to make. I thought about continuing home, and I thought about Cade. He was suffering, and I owed him a lot. I was sure he wouldn't have seen it that way, but he'd accepted me, treating me like an equal on the case when few others would.

I texted Lucio: I have unfinished business here. Giovanni will have to wait.

And then I called Cade.

"I'm not letting you go through this alone," I said. "I'll see you in an hour."

I steered the car to the next exit and then turned around. On the drive back to Jackson Hole, I thought about my life, what I wanted, what I needed, and where I was going. I didn't know, really. All I could see was the day in front of me and where it would take me: back into the life of a new friend.

For updates on the author
and her books:

Blog: cherylbradshawbooks.blogspot.com
Web: cherylbradshaw.com
Facebook: Cheryl Bradshaw Books
Twitter: @cherylbradshaw

All of Cheryl Bradshaw's novels are heavily researched, proofed, edited, and professionally formatted. Should you find any errors, please contact the author directly. Her assistant will forward the issue(s) to the publisher. It's our goal to present you with the best possible reading experience, and we appreciate your help in making that happen. You can contact the author through her website, www.cherylbradshaw.com.

AFTERWORD

What you have just read is a work of fiction, but unfortunately, the type of kidnapping described in the novel exists in the world today.

According to recent statistics, more than 800,000 children under the age of eighteen are reported missing each year. That amounts to almost 2,200 per day. What I am about to say might be a bit hard for you to read, so if you are sensitive, I'd advise you to stop reading now.

Similar to what I wrote about in Stranger in Town, children are sometimes taken by illegal agencies. They put the children up for adoption or for sale. Kidnappers working for the agency may even be asked to find a specific type of child. But that's not all.

Children are sometimes taken for their organs. In society today, people can even search the internet for a broker and pay a price for the organ they desire. It's hard to believe, but it's true, and it's a multi-million dollar criminal industry, surpassing all others in profitability, even drug smuggling.

In many countries children are even sold into prostitution, many men preferring young, white, blond girls. Boys might also be taken for breeding purposes. Over a million children are bought and sold across international borders every single year. Most are sold into the commercial sex trade.

Human trafficking is horrific, but nonetheless real. To learn how you can help prevent these crimes, check out the Operation61 website, www.operation61.org.

CPSIA information can be obtained
at www.ICGtesting.com
Printed in the USA
LVHW02s1032220818
587248LV00001B/82/P